NO ORDINARY JOE

NO ORDINARY JOE

Siobhán Daffy

NO ORDINARY JOE

First published in 2021 by
Little Island Books
7 Kenilworth Park
Dublin 6W
Ireland

ISBN: 978-1-912417-77-3

Cover illustration by Dan Bramall
Typeset and design by Nolan Book Design
Copyedited and proofread by Emma Dunne

Printed in Poland by Drukarnia Skleniarz

Little Island receives financial support from
the Arts Council/An Chomhairle Ealaíon

10 9 8 7 6 5 4 3 2 1

For Donnacha

SATURDAY

The Field

What do you usually do on Saturday mornings? I bet you like to lie in bed, snug under the covers with the duvet pulled over your ears. Or maybe you like to watch TV, stretched out on the couch with a bowl of cereal within easy reach? I bet you do not have to chase your brother through a muddy field. I bet you don't. I could be wrong, of course. But I'm willing to bet you were toasty in bed reading a good book while I was out of breath already from making my way across Mr Maloney's long field.

It's impossible to run in wellies, especially when it's raining. My feet were slurped into the fragrant brown–green pools of cow poo, like giant suckers. It's like musical farts.

SQUELCH

SLURP

SQUELCH

SLURP　　SQUELCH　　SLURP

SQUELCH

Mr Maloney's field is a fiendish obstacle course of grassy hillocks, pitted holes, cow-pats and muck. My raincoat was flapping around my legs like Granny's nightdress. With no time to lose, I'd grabbed the first one that came to hand. I think it used to be Mam's. Half the poppers are broken on the bottom end. You can't be too fashion-conscious on this mission. You've just got to hope no-one has a phone out, looking for an Insta moment. I'm sure I looked like a nutcase leaping around the place, an enormous crow tossed about in the wind. This could be one for *I'm a Celebrity – The Ultimate Challenge.*

Can you survive?
Pitted against a barrage of stinking cow-pats,
blasts of wind and driving rain.
All costumes provided – saggy green wellies up past your knees
and your mam's old raincoat.

I bet it would be a roaring success. I'd need a hot feed at the end of this. I hoped Kit would keep her word on the pancakes. I don't know how Joe runs so fast. My one and only brother. Currently haring along the bottom end of the field, brandishing a long stick, in hot pursuit of a herd of Friesian cattle. I was thinking, if I headed him off before the water trough I could get both of us back home as quickly as possible and out of the pouring rain. That's the strategy that was unfolding in my head while I was dodging cow-pats.

Unfortunately,
he had other ideas.

My sister, Kit, had spotted him first. She'd handed me the binoculars with a groan, saying, 'It's your turn to do the field, Dan.'

Nightmare. As far as she's concerned it's always my turn to do the field. The road is more dangerous, but most of the time he prefers the field. He just can't resist the cows. By the time we've noticed he's missing he'll usually have helped himself to a nice long branch and be tearing after them like a speeding bullet. He loves the chase. In another life he'd have been a cowboy on a ranch in Texas.

You have to sneak up behind him or you risk getting trampled by the stampede coming the other way. He never wants to be caught, so if he sees you coming, he'll take off in the opposite direction, and no amount of shouting makes any difference. I tried to stick close to the middle hedge, out of view of the farm, so Mr Maloney wouldn't be coming over to moan about his darling cows losing their beauty sleep. I mean, he's pretty understanding, all things considered, but I had no time then for a detailed discussion on unusual summer weather while the rain was trickling down my neck and leaking into my socks.

Mr Maloney is rainproof, waterproof, impervious. Seriously. No matter how bad it's storming and pouring, his waxed coat stays polished and straight, his hair welded in place so you can see the individual strands shining on his baldy head. He stands in the rain, yakking away as if there's nothing going on at all.

There's Joe. I could just make him out in the distance, a tiny speck of red flickering amongst the running cows.

Who needs the rodeo? You can have it any day around here. I was gaining on him, but he's fast and the wellies were tripping me up. There's no way I was wearing my new Nike trainers, though: one trip through here and that would be the end of them.

Joe has lost so many pairs of shoes, we've lost count. They come off in the marsh of cow muck over by the drinking troughs where it's deepest and most stinking.

I wanted to catch him before he hit it or I'd be half an hour poking at the swamp looking for his blasted runners.

Kit refuses to cross it any more, even in wellies. She practically tiptoes through the field, holding her dress like a Victorian lady. But I remember when she used to peg it around like the rest of us. Turning seventeen will do that to you. She won't climb trees either, but she used to hang from the top of the evergreen and just let go. Now she's a hopeless case. She's either lost in a forest of exam notes or admiring herself in the mirror. There's no in between. It's completely sickening.

Blast it! I was getting totally drenched. I wasn't even properly dressed. I'd my pyjamas rolled into the legs of the wellies. I could feel them slowly soaking up the rain. The wind drove it in around my legs and the raincoat was useless, all six foot of it.

He really picks his moments, Joe. I was all set for vegging out in front of the telly this morning. He doesn't check the weather forecast and think, *I'll give the jailbreak a miss this morning and cosy up on the couch.* He's not the genius type of special needs, my brother. He's the type whose brain is not working properly. So even though he is eleven he behaves like he's two. Although I don't know any two-year-olds who chase cows, so let's just say he has his own way of doing things. Sometimes this can have its embarrassing moments, of course. But as Mam says, nobody's perfect.

I had him cornered now. He knew the game was up and he was losing juice. At long last! We were like two drowned rats. Dad would have to stick him in the bath when we got in. He was covered in cow poo and he stank. Mr Maloney's cows are all organic, but that doesn't make them smell any better. At least he had both his shoes, even if they needed urgent medical attention. They were firmly stuck on his feet and that's what matters. He gave me one of his massive grins and kept a firm hold on the stick.

'Moo cow,' he said.

He knew the game was up, but he wasn't relinquishing his sword. I couldn't be bothered being mad with him.

I grabbed him by the hand and we squelched our way back uphill, through the minefield of cow-pats, to climb over the wall in a ramshackle heap and trample up the road to our house.

'In our house you have to think on your toes,' Dad says. This doesn't mean standing on your toes while you're thinking. It means being able to think up a plan in an emergency, because you never know when an emergency might arrive. We are never far from an unexpected situation. You can't plan for what might happen next so you have to think on your toes.

5

Most of the unexpected situations have to do with my brother, Joe. Mam says he keeps us on our toes. I reckon my parents are obsessed with feet. She means we don't get much time for lounging around because Joe is not big into relaxation. My brother didn't come with a map. We have to figure it out as we go along. You can't tell by looking at a tiny baby what the map of their life is going to be. No-one knows if they'll be mad for chasing cows or if they'll invent an electric plane.

If you were to meet Joe on the street, for a second you might think he was just the same as me or you. He has carrot-red hair and blue eyes that stare right through you. He walks a bit funny, so if you were the detective type you might spot straight away he's a bit unusual. He kind of moves sideways, like a crab, instead of straight ahead and he's *not* very good at waiting.

For anything.
He's always rocketing on
to the next thing.

Patience is not his strong suit. I'm with him on that one – to a point. It can get a bit frustrating when you spend ages waiting for something to happen, like Christmas. He'll badger you about it every day non-stop for months, then as soon as it arrives, he's looking for the next thing. For example, with presents, he could be pure obsessed about getting a new truck to the point where everyone is driven demented because he won't talk about anything else.

It's like

truck   truck   truck   truck   truck
truck

truck truck truck

truck   truck   truck   truck
truck   truck

mah truck

truck truck

when mah truck?

Santa truck?

Truck   truck   truck   truck   truck.

Even when it's only September.

But when Christmas *finally* comes, he'll take one look at his presents and start messing with *my* stuff or following me around trying to get my guitar.

That was one present he didn't
put down.
He loves his guitar. Now he can 'play', just like me.

My brother Joe doesn't *get* the way you're supposed to act in shops or on the street or in the cinema. If there's an exciting bit in a film he might jump up and start shouting and pointing his fingers like a gun. Or he might decide to sing along. He never sings quietly either. He shouts, belting out the words he recognises, usually just a couple. He doesn't care what anyone thinks or whether the movie is still running. He lives in his own world and it has different rules to our world. There's no point trying to make him stick to our rules all the time. He's just not able. Everyone ends up tetchy and upset. Besides, some of our rules are kind of stupid. Why shouldn't you jump up and start singing if you feel excited? They do it in musicals all the time. But if you behave like that in real life you get funny looks and everyone thinks you're bonkers. Our world can be a bit boring. His world has more action. There's always something going on.

If you didn't know my brother, you could think he was just a bit thick. You're not supposed to call people thick because it's not polite. But people do. It's mostly because they can't understand his world or why he does strange things. Most of the time we don't understand it either.

We're all practising *acceptance* in our house. Acceptance is where you love someone *exactly how they are* and don't keep trying to make them act the way *you* think they should. It sounds easy but actually it's really hard, especially if you're with that person all the time.

Mam spends a lot of her time tearing around after Joe. She jokes that she could have bought a racehorse instead. No kidding. He's got so fast she can't catch him any more, so she usually gets me to do the chasing. I'm pretty fast. I play centre-forward on the hurling team. I used to do football too but it clashed with guitar. Hurling is great but what keeps me fittest is chasing my brother.

Dad says I should take him to school and cure the obesity problem. They wouldn't know what to make of him in my class.

Joe has superhero skills most people don't recognise.

For a start, he's the best escape artist I know. We put a new fence around the garden because he's so good at climbing and escaping. Mam is petrified he'll break a leg or an arm. He's not so skilled at scaling trees; he can be a bit clumsy even though he's excellent at escapes. Even with the new fence you have to keep your eyes peeled or he'll be off like a hot snot. The field behind our house is one of his top-three escapes. Dad keeps a set of binoculars on the windowsill upstairs so we can pinpoint his location. Even without binoculars I can always tell by the stampede of cows haring across the field. Then one of us is dispatched into the mud and cow poo to fetch him home.

When I say *one of us*, it's ninety-nine per cent me. As I explained before, Kit is now allergic to the field. She says it's because she's doing exams. She has everyone convinced it's interrupting her study time but she doesn't mind cycling down the road. It's highly unfair. The real reason is she doesn't want to chip her nails on the wall or tear her designer jeans on the barbed wire fence. And she wouldn't be seen dead in a pair of green wellies.

Nadia across the road says Kit has a crush on Tommy K. This would be very tragic, as Tommy K is a complete loser in my esteemed opinion. But according to Kit, my opinion is just my opinion. It's not worth a fig in the big bad world. She also says she doesn't fancy Tommy K, but she won't agree that he's a loser.

Everyone thinks he's great because he's the king of sport. Star player, super-scorer, man of the match. They say he's never lost a match. I'm sure that's a wild exaggeration. He really thinks he's something special but he's not been in my top ten since I heard him slagging off my brother outside the Spar last summer. Dad was in there trying to stop Joe from raiding the sweets beside the till. What do they expect when they stack the loot in pretty rows exactly where he can reach? Anyway, he was throwing a classic wobbler in the shop, trying to grab a handful of Skittles. (He really loves Skittles but the colours drive him mental.) Dad was trying to wrestle him out the door. He sent me ahead with the bags of shopping. I was trying to haul them to the car, chasing a renegade tin of tomatoes, when I heard Tommy making his nasty remarks.

'Watch out for slow Joe,' he said with a laugh. And he started imitating Joe's voice, the way he talks.

People can't help staring sometimes. I suppose I'd stare myself if I wasn't so used to him, but there's no need to be mean. There's no need to be *cruel*. Since that day I can't stand TK no matter how many medals he's won. He's a giant slime ball, plain and simple.

And that's my last word on the matter.

So this morning, Dad had the bath ready by the time we got back from the field. I stripped Joe off at the back door. You couldn't see his runners for the mud, so I left them sitting in the grass, hoping the rain would take care of them.

'Eye-ceem,' said Joe hopefully as we burst in the kitchen door.

'Not now, Joe.'

The cow-poo smell was stinking up my nose and I couldn't get him in the bath fast enough.

'Eye-ceem' is his word for ice cream. Anyone who knows him knows what he means. Some words he can say, like 'truck' (which admittedly comes out more like 'tuck'), but some words he just can't.

He's totally crazy about eye-ceem. It's his absolute top favourite. Any flavour will do, but the best is a classic cone from one of the ice-cream machines – a ninety-nine with a chocolate Flake and raspberry syrup on top. Those really rock his world. The only problem is he loves the cone so much that he bites the bottom straight off, and all the ice cream leaks out the end. Even though we try and stop him, this happens nearly every time he eats one. Then it's melted ice cream dripping all over his face and his clothes and the car, full-on ice-cream tsunami.

Dad goes mental about the car seats. He says our car looks like the inside of a dustbin. He's not exaggerating. There are probably hundreds of ice creams melted into that back seat, and popcorn goes everywhere, no matter how careful you try to be. I know this because it's always me who ends up squished in the bottom of the car with the skinny end of the hoover trying to suck up weeks of dirt. Dad reckons he's too tall to get in there but I'm pretty sure he could manage if he tried. It's my worst nightmare job after sorting socks.

Joe hates not being allowed to have eye-ceem, but you can't let him have it every time he asks. It's not good for him. It's strictly for treats. He's not allowed too much milk either. But if you don't race him to the fridge he can have half a carton gone before you reach the door. He's supposed to drink rice milk but it doesn't taste as good. Who can blame him? We have crates of the stuff and no-one fights him for it. We're forever running out of cow's milk, which is kind of funny, considering the house is surrounded by cows.

Granny brings her own milk because, she says, the tea is not the same with rice milk. Granny likes her traditions. She's probably right. I'm not a big tea drinker but cornflakes are not the same with rice milk either. I've just given up caring.

We are sadly used to rabbit food, as Kit calls it. It's carrot sticks and apple slices all the way here. Don't rock up expecting fizzy drinks and Mars bars, or you'll be sadly disappointed. (Unless you bring your own biscuits.) We love visitors because they always break the rules. There's a ban on processed crap. Treats are only on the weekends or else you have to keep them hidden in your room. And when I say hidden, I mean dig a six-foot hole – don't just leave them in your underwear drawer.

'If my granny wouldn't recognise it as food, it's not for us.' That's Mam's rule of thumb.

My brother isn't officially allergic to anything. It won't kill him if he eats processed food, but some foods just make him hyper or sick. All our vegetables come from Butterfly Farm. Pure organic. They don't spray them with any big bad chemicals. Our vegetables are like the odd-sock drawer: none of them make pairs. Carrots don't always come in long, straight lines. Our cucumbers are knobbly and twisted.

'You wouldn't pour toilet cleaner in your soup,' says Mr Maloney, 'so why would you spray it on your broccoli?'

It's a fair point.

By the time we got Joe dried and dressed, Kit had made an enormous mound of pancakes. We were just finished eating when the doorbell rang. My best friend, Lucas, usually cycles over on the weekends.

'Pay game,' said Joe the minute he saw Lucas. He means *play* game.

Usually we head out on the bikes. But the rain was still bucketing down so Lucas had brought his games console.

It's just as well Dad was taking Joe to his horse-riding group. Joe is a disaster on the PlayStation. He pulls at the controls but he can't make them work and he tries to stop us playing. Once he hid a game so well that we bought Lucas a new one because it didn't turn up for months. Lucas tries to be kind to Joe but he doesn't like him interfering all the time. I always let Joe have a go but Lucas gets annoyed. He doesn't have any younger brothers. In his house no-one interrupts you when you're playing games. Every house is different.

'Have fun at the horse riding, cowboy,' Lucas called as he dived on the couch and threw a bag of sweets in my direction.

I reckon there's a ninja hiding in our kitchen, messing with the clock. Whenever I'm doing jobs, time creeps by in milliseconds, but as soon as Lucas and I are playing video games, it only feels like five minutes

until Dad and Joe come
bursting back in the door.

On Saturdays me and Dad are on dinner duty. Kit is off the hook 'cos she is in the middle of exams. More excuses!

Her last exam is on Thursday. I can't wait. We'll all be extremely relieved when it's over. Kit spends hours in her room studying and being stressed. Of course, no-one has any proof that's what she's really doing. She could be sleeping in there or eating her way through a clandestine mound of chocolate. She has a secret stash in a box in her bedside locker. I know where she keeps it.

She has a big highlighter collection, yards of flash cards and a rake of sticky notes stuck to her wall with hints for the exams. She wants to be a brain surgeon so she can operate on malfunctioning brains. In biology she had to dissect a sheep's heart. I think that's disgusting, but Kit doesn't mind gore: her favourite movies are the zombie horrors where people fall around with their guts hanging out and half their heads eaten. Gruesome. Compared to that, dissecting a sheep heart is easy-peasy.

We were supposed to be making chickpea curry but we ran out of chickpeas so we made mashed potatoes, eggs and beans instead. Does that sound too simple? Too processed? You betcha. Don't forget the …

lightly steamed kale and broccoli on the side
or the grated carrot, beetroot and apple salad
with toasted seeds

What did I tell you?

No matter what I do, dinners in this house are always very *green* and very *crunchy*. Beans apparently don't count as a vegetable, as they come out of a tin and are full of sugar, but we all love them. (Especially Joe, who isn't a fan of the grated carrot, no matter where it appears.)

Making dinner with Dad has its good points. He sings along to the radio while he cooks, using the wooden spoons as drumsticks. I peel potatoes; that's my job. Peel the spuds, grate the carrots. I'm an oiled machine –

Peel peel

Chop chop chop

Grate grate grate grate

Joe wandered in and out of the house, twirling his stick. He needs a lot of outside time. Even if it's lashing rain he goes out. He walks around and around the garden telling the stories of his day. He chats away to himself while he's walking. He can't tell anyone else what's happened so he tells himself the whole story over and over. At least that's what it sounds like to me. I kept one eye out the window while grating beetroot in case he made a run for it. Mam works late on Saturdays. She'd go mental if we let him escape again. And I didn't fancy another trek across the field.

Saturday night is movie night *if* we can all agree on something. As you can imagine, this can take a while. Dad and Kit love the horrors, the gorier the better. Mam likes the weird ones in foreign languages where no-one has a clue what's going on. Joe and I are always on for some shootout action, but Mam hates us watching violence. Everyone loves a good comedy. Dad makes popcorn and sometimes I make buns or Kit bakes flapjacks when she gets home.

Nobody bothers with early nights at the weekend, but someone always has to get up with Joe so we've a rota for morning patrol. It's rota city here – lists for everything and charts with little boxes to fill up with names for the laundry and the clean-up, the recycling, the dinners and the morning patrol. Mam is into lists. Even if they get lost or everyone forgets, she feels better once there's a list made. I reckon she hopes that when our names go into the little boxes on the rota chart, everything will magically become more organised. Sadly it doesn't always work that way. We couldn't find the rota for Sunday morning so guess who volunteered to get up? Sometimes it's easier to volunteer than to argue.

And Joe loves a good pillow fight before breakfast.

SUNDAY

An Enormous Pigeon

I don't know about time machines, but sometimes I get to Sunday and I reckon it's been at least a month since Monday.

Joe beat me to the kitchen. There was a bit of an incident with one of the pillows. By the time I made it in the door he was sitting on the floor with a box of cornflakes spilled over the tiles. What did I tell you, super-speed! He wasn't even eating them. He was playing with them, grinding them into the floor. It was too late to salvage any.

'No bold,' he said.

He looked up at me with his puppy-dog eyes.

He meant, *I don't want to be bold even though I know I'm not supposed to pour cornflakes on the floor.*

'Let's give them to the birds,' I said.

So we piled the cornflake crumbs on the bird table in little heaps. It's their lucky day. They have it good, the birds in our garden; it could be peanut butter toast tomorrow. Joe looked disappointed when I spooned porridge into his bowl. He doesn't really think things out. He loves cornflakes on Sundays; it's porridge the whole rest of the week.

I put on some music while I tidied up. Joe is mad for Christmas songs but I didn't give in. Once you start with the Christmas songs he'll keep asking, non-stop. Not many things bother me, but singing 'Santa Claus Is Coming to Town' when it's nearly July is just *wrong*.

Luckily there are plenty of other choices. Dad makes lots of playlists for Joe. He loves music; he tries his best at dancing and singing along. He can't say the words right so his singing is all jumbled up but we know what he means. His favourite song is 'Hey Jude'. He's a bit retro that way. He likes all the rest of the Beatles as well and Van Morrison, Queen and Paul Simon – that's because of my dad. He doesn't like Iron Maiden, though. When they play he grinds his teeth and holds his head, which must be saying something about their music.

My dad won't hear any negative remarks. Iron Maiden reminds him of when he was young and had no children. Now he's fifty and ancient. He has a round bald patch on the top of his head that he tries to cover up but you don't have to look very hard to find it.

Then there's *my* music. I'm going to be a famous guitar player one day. Joe is my greatest fan so far, but Nadia across the road will ask for a request when no-one is looking, so I reckon I can count her as well.

'Any new songs?' she asks whenever she calls over.

She gives me this serious look with her brown–black eyes, like she genuinely wants to know. I can almost play 'Blackbird', which is a tricky song, but I practise every day. Joe has his own guitar so he can pretend-play. His hands can't manage strumming and he can't remember any chords but when he's sitting with me playing guitar, he is pure delighted.

Dad says I should learn 'House of the Rising Sun', which he started with when he was learning but I've got other plans.

I'm writing my own songs and it's guaranteed they'll be smash hits because I'm an unstoppable force. Everyone says so. Well, not everyone. I might be lying a bit about that. Granny says I am inclined to stretch the truth.

Even if it's just breakfast, the kitchen always looks as though a cyclone has been through after Joe. I was under the table with the brush and dustpan when I saw Mam's strappy sandals making their way downstairs. She was all ready for mass. Her hair was pinned up and she had a flowery dress on. Joe is religious whether he likes it or not. Mostly I go along too. Sometimes I meet Lucas at the shops afterwards. If there's a match on, his dad might take us both.

Joe hates sitting still, so mass is his worst nightmare. But he likes knowing the same thing is happening each week, so at least it's a predictable nightmare. Once he's there he fidgets and pokes at me and talks to himself. Sometimes people give him dirty looks, but Mam says God's house is for everyone, no matter what.

Some of the teachers at Joe's school go too. He loves seeing them all. Even though he's just seen them on Friday, he gets all excited. Of course, he can't talk to anyone during the mass, so the best part for Joe is when all the official stuff is over. Then he gets to run around outside and say hello/ goodbye to everyone. It's a fun experience once he doesn't have to stay still or be quiet.

Mam had his good clothes ironed and folded over her arm. Joe's good clothes are always the very last things to go on, so you know they'll still be clean going out the door.

'Where's Joe?' she asked.

'Dancing to his songs,' I said, glancing across to the sitting room.

There was no-one there.

'Well he's not there now!' She walked out of the kitchen. I could hear her sandals click-clicking down the hall.

'He was there a second ago.'

I scanned the room. His stick was still on the couch. I never heard him go. Talk about superhero stealth – when he wants, he can move without a sound.

The amazing
inaudible
invisible
vanishing
boy

Now you see him –
Now you don't!

Mam's feet were click-clicking back up the hall, gathering speed. 'The doors are still locked. He must be in the house,' she said.

I remembered the cornflakes. She caught me looking out at the bird table.

'We might have opened the back door,' I said quietly.

'Did you lock it again, Dan?'

'He didn't go out, Mam. I know he didn't.'

'Did you lock the door again, Dan?'

I shook my head.

She ran and shouted up the stairs: 'Has anyone seen Joe?'

That put a sharp end to the Sunday morning lie-in. I could hear them stumbling sleepily, like elephants waking up in the jungle. I ran upstairs to grab the binoculars. Dad was on the landing in his underpants, a hazy mirage of aftershave and steam. Kit was firing clothes around, searching for her jeans. Kit doesn't do mornings. It's best to keep out of her way until the sun is high in the sky.

Dad looked at me. 'Any sign?' he asked.

'Negative,' I replied.

I took up my post at the bedroom window. I scanned Mr Maloney's hedges and the surrounding fields, checking for any movement in the herd.

That's when I heard Mam shriek. Then stop. Kit tore down the stairs. But soon after I saw her tiptoe back up to the window at the end of the landing. *What's she doing?* I wondered. She pulled the curtains carefully.

Joe was sitting outside on the windowsill, looking down, like an enormous pigeon.

Everyone stood frozen to the spot, afraid to move in case it gave him the same idea. The window was wide open. He was perched on the ledge. I could hear Mam outside speaking in her calm voice. Dad unstuck his feet and made a dash for it.

'Don't move, buddy!' he called.

He reached out and caught Joe's arm. Kit inched over and stroked his fingers. I was afraid to watch, so I made my way downstairs.

Outside in the garden, Mam was standing in the flower-bed looking up.

'Dad will help you climb back inside,' she was saying up to Joe. 'Can you move a bit more that way, Joe?'

She waved her hand helplessly to where Dad and Kit were standing inside.

But Joe didn't know how to manoeuvre himself. He was stuck.

'Will I call the fire brigade?' a familiar voice said.

Nadia from across the road was standing behind me, looking up.

She's always doing that, creeping up behind me like a super-scout so I don't hear her coming. She's practising extra stealth for when she gets to visit the rainforest.

'A ladder!' said Mam. 'Good idea, Nadia. Can you give me a hand? Stay there, Dan.'

She threw open the garage door, chucked off her strappy sandals and started unearthing a mound of junk so she could move the ladder. They carried it together to the wall. Then she went inside and swopped places with Dad. I never realised ladders were so heavy – it looks so easy in the movies. Dad pushed it high against the wall and climbed up. But Joe didn't want to climb back down; he's not really able for ladders. In the end, Kit went and got an ice cream and they eventually lured him back in the window.

'It's OK, Dan, you can look now,' Nadia said.

It was only then I realised my hands were over my eyes.

'I guess we need to put a safety lock on that one,' I said, trying to stop my voice from shaking.

Nadia pretended not to notice. She knows about the windows. Joe's bedroom window is permanently locked so he can't get out there. Dad locked it up after he dismantled his bedside table one time and shoved it out, lock, stock and barrel.

We're used to his tricks. Last week he fired a load of my Lego Technic out the bathroom window. The trouble with the bathroom window is you can't reach that part of the roof very easily. It took me ages to get it down. All the tiny pieces were stuck in the gutter. I nearly broke the drainpipe. Dad said I wasn't allowed to climb on the roof but that's ridiculous – how else am I supposed to rescue my stuff?

Kit and Nadia hit the kitchen and started a pot of hot chocolate. Mam went to change her clothes. That was kind of cool, the way she threw off her heels and laid into the junk. I can see where Joe gets his superhero genes. Mass must have been half-over by the time we were sitting down with mugs of steaming hot chocolate. I'm sure God takes it into account if you have a genuine emergency.

Granny came directly from the church, dying to know what had delayed us. Mam opened the door.

'Joe went for a bit of a wander,' she said before anyone else could get a word in. 'Nothing to worry about, we were just delayed. There was no point in going.'

'You'd need eyes in the back of your head, Lorna,' Granny said, pouring herself a milky cup of tea while giving Joe a disapproving look.

Joe is completely immune to disapproving looks.

Granny is not able for my brother. She doesn't mean any

harm by it; she does her best. She's just not able to keep up with him. If we go to Granny's I have to be on duty all the time. Sometimes if I'm distracted by comic books, it doesn't always work out.

There was a bit of an incident with the geraniums.

And the glass cabinet.

And the pavlova.

That last incident was Granny's own fault. Everyone knows Joe will stop at nothing if it concerns dessert or cake. If we bake a cake for a special occasion, Mam hides it in the utility room until it's time to eat it. The kitchen has a sliding door to the sitting room, which is a bit of an issue in our house. Sliding doors are easily overcome and open quietly.

It's not like he takes a tiny slice or a lick off the side, like the rest of us would do, when no-one's looking. Nobody would notice that. His usual thing is to stick his fist straight into the whole creamy mess and eat the top off. That never goes down well. Kit made a special cake for Mam's birthday a few weeks ago and forgot to hide it. Joe was on it in a flash. She really flipped the lid because she'd spent ages decorating it and peeling papaya, which it turns out is not that easy. We salvaged what we could. It looked a mess, but it's the taste that counts, right?

You kind of need a SWAT team busting in ahead of Joe to get the cakes, the sugar bowl, the valuable crockery and the pot plants out of the way. As Granny has sadly discovered, Joe does not have any love for pot plants. They mostly wind up upside down in a heap with the soil mashed into the floor and the roots tangled up in knots.

I know this from personal experience. I've spent hundreds of Sunday afternoons untangling roots and scooping loose piles of soil back into pots. They never look right, no matter how carefully I try to piece them back together. Granny can always tell. She puts the trailing ones up high, but that can be bad news too. Joe will just reach up, grab them by the tail and pull. Disaster. Mam says we'll stick to garden flowers, but you can't expect every house to do the same. And anyway, garden flowers mostly wind up with the heads pulled off: a bunch of bare stalks sitting in the sun.

As you can imagine, we've no SWAT team. I'm the entire team rolled into one. I even asked Mam to get me one of those SWAT-team jackets for Halloween last year but she didn't go for it. Not enough creativity involved. Out came the sewing machine and the cornflakes box. Kill-joy. Just once could I buy a fearsome disguise instead of stapling my fingers to a cardboard box?

In the end Kit came to the rescue. She's got skills. I was a cereal killer in a giant box of cornflakes. Cereal killer! Call me cheesy but I loved it. I won best costume at scouts so it was worth the effort in the end. Best costume was awarded a giant bag of M&Ms, my absolute favourite. Kit took a few for tax but no-one else dared to put their hand out. I'm like a grizzly bear coming out of hibernation when it comes to M&Ms.

Sometimes it's worth the effort to go homemade. We're a major DIY house. The garden shed is like a shrine to adhesive. Wood glue, PVA, Super Glue, ceramic Super Stik – you name it, we've got it. Whatever is broken, Dad will give it a go. He's an eternal optimist. If your leg was hanging on by a single thread, he'd be, like, 'Hold on there now, we'll have it stuck back in a jiffy.' There's nothing Dad won't try to glue back together. He always has a stack of construction projects on the go: bedside table, bookshelves, shoe rack, you name it. Plus a long list of unfinished jobs he's supposed to be working on at the weekends.

The trouble is, weekends are pretty chock-a-block. Whenever Mam threatens a trip to IKEA, Dad gets the toolbox out. It's like he finds the word offensive. Last time he went on a bender I got a study table for my room with bookshelves overhead. It's pretty cool.

He lets me do the sanding and the screws as long as Joe's hands are kept busy. Joe's pretty lethal with a hammer. Last time he ran away with one, I lost an entire Lego spaceship and a radio tower before I could get it back off him.

Crunch
    splat
crunch
    splat
crunch.

The end.

It was that quick.

I admit it's very satisfying the way it crumbles so quickly. If it hadn't been so hard to build I would've enjoyed smashing it myself. 'The whole point of Lego is that you can build it again.' That's what Dad said. Easy for him to say – he didn't spend hours putting it together.

Oh, well. I've given up complaining to Joe. He hates when I give out to him. He gives me *the sad look*. After *the sad look* I can't go on being mad. When I'm really BOILING mad I go and throw logs at the woodpile. At least with the woodpile it can't shout back at you. And when you're done, you're done. You can walk away from the woodpile knowing you're safe from repercussions. It's not going to sneak after you into the house and fire a log at the back of your head when you least expect it.

Usually I hate Sunday evenings, but not this one. There's only one more week of school to go. Summer holidays are so close I can smell them. Just like you can smell the ocean as you get near. Isn't that the best smell? Salty air and soft sand as you run over the dunes for the first view of the crashing waves. Best feeling ever. It's always tricky on the beach with Joe, in case he runs off, but I hope we can go during the holidays. I can't wait one second more.

My legs are allergic to getting up in the morning. Dad says I've a case of school-itis, that it's common this time of year. Now I know how Joe feels, tearing off over the hedge. I'm like a horse in a stable dying to gallop through the fields. It's the smell. Everything smells of summer –

soft piles of cut grass,
        bright yellow sunshine,
                white lilac petals falling on the road,
                        sticky orange ice pops down at the Spar.

It's the smell of the long evenings when daytime stretches and stretches for ever. Already it's so bright we can play outside till eleven. It's impossible to sleep. Even if you pull the curtains, light creeps in around the edges and you can hear happy voices echoing across the fields. Then you know for certain that no-one else is stupid enough to try and sleep, so why bother trying?

MONDAY

Draniki

In my dream I'm tearing across the pitch, just about to score a goal.

Then suddenly I'm awake. And Dad is standing over me with an armload of tops looking for one with a label. Mam and Kit have already left. Dad is a hopeless case when it comes to laundry.

All Joe's clothes have little white labels with his name on. He never remembers his clothes. The labels make it easier to locate them in other people's houses or in school. Every time he gets new clothes Mam gets out the sewing kit and stitches on a label. Some things make their way back. Some are lost for ever.

'You can put labels on people as well as clothes,' Mam says. 'Don't be so quick to judge; you don't know that person's story. Walk a mile in their shoes – then you might have some idea.'

She doesn't mean literally stomping around in some lady's high heels. She means, *Imagine if you were in that life, being that person.* I don't know if I could handle a mile in Joe's shoes. It would drive me mad, everyone telling me what to do and chasing after me. So what if he wants to tear around the field chasing cows? But no-one wants him to get hurt.

And then there are the cows to consider. If you were to walk
a mile in their shoes, how would that be?

> All sorts of labels are put on my brother
> but that doesn't mean he's any one thing.

> At the end of the day, they're just words.
> A pile of letters pooled together.

shdfjshgfsjhgfmisutarnairgedamedlnteyaldeshjgfsjhfg

> You can jumble up the letters in those words
> any way you want –
> they still won't spell his name.

None of those words will find him when he's running away.
None of those words will pinpoint his shoes in the mud.
None of those words will play his guitar.

The thing is, no two people are exactly alike. There are
identical twins in my class. I mean, they *look* identical but
Amy's a complete bookworm and Rosie is football all the
way – she hates reading. The way I see it everyone has their
own story; no two stories are the same. But if you don't get
to know them you might never find out.

In school my teacher, Ms Fox, has these new robot things
for learning maths. She wanted us to figure them out for
the younger classes. At least that's what she said. We spent
the whole day playing with the things. You can tell it's the
last week of school. I'm not a big fan of teachers but Ms Fox
scores pretty high in the stakes.

There are two main reasons for this:

1. She never shouts.
2. When things go wrong, she always listens. She wants to know what happened and what you would have done differently. It's called restorative practice.

Last year I was unlucky with Cruella Crab, who was forever shouting at people, 'BE QUIET.'

'Some people aren't cut out for teaching,' Mam says.

She knows all about it. She teaches adults at the local college. Apparently you need a lot of patience. But Mam loves it; she never gets bored.

Joe pretends he'll be going to secondary school with me in September. We all know it's just a game, but he loves it. He wouldn't last a second in there. He goes to a different school, where he swims in a warm pool to stretch his muscles. He loves swimming, but he's not really the competitive type, unless it's against the cows in the field next door. I don't think he'll ever learn to read. He can't talk properly, so reading is out of the question.

Most days I cycle to school. Kit gets the bus. Dad drops Joe to school on his way to work. Joe's school is the furthest away, in a big centre where they do residential care and classes for people with disabilities. It's a maze of a building and it smells a bit like a hospital. There's loads of ramps and automatic doors 'cos lots of the kids are in wheelchairs. Joe loves horsing about making the doors open and close, but you have to duck out of sight so the staff can't spot you on the CCTV. The centre has big grounds with a huge willow tree you can hide under and a big tall wall all the way around. It used to be a laundry run by nuns for girls who were sent away from their families. They spent their whole lives washing sheets. Mam says it was a terrible place back then; it was like being sent to prison.

But now there are sunflowers painted all over the walls and Joe's teachers are the best. He loves them all, especially Brian. Brian plays guitar and sings rock songs. He learned 'Hey Jude' especially so he could play it for Joe. Brian knows all his favourite foods and he knows to keep the sugar bowl under wraps. He knows Joe loves getting his feet massaged in the chill-out room. And he takes him for long walks around the grounds so he can tire him out. Joe never gets tired out, but walks are always popular, so Brian can't go wrong on that score. I'm not entirely sure what he does the rest of the time. Some days he brings back a painting or a little pot with a tiny seed planted for a sunflower to grow. Those generally don't survive the journey home.

Cycling home from school is the best. Especially when there's no homework and the sun is shining. Nadia races me from the top of the road. Our road is called Beech Road, because of all the beech trees. At the bottom end is Mr Maloney's farm; his fields run along by the wall. At the top end, beside the bottle bank, is Old Mrs Turner.

Old Mrs Turner lives with her son Philip in a stone cottage covered in roses. It looks like a gingerbread cottage, but sadly it's made of stones instead of sweets. Philip mows the lawn and keeps the roses clipped, while Old Mrs Turner sits in her garden chair and keeps an eye on who is passing up and down the road. She has a tiny brown dog, Maisie, who would be cute except for her annoying yappy bark. She likes to chase you if you're on a bike. She's a total pain in the neck but you can't complain in front of Mrs Turner.

Halfway up the road is our house and Nadia's is directly opposite. Nadia has a slime factory in her garden shed. She's going to be a crazy scientist some day and invent a way to save the environment. She says you can make plastic from banana skins. She has her own bench full of washing-up liquid, glue, shampoo, flour and other things that make the best slime. She used to make it in the house, until her mother banned it because it kept turning up on the kitchen ceiling. I'm not that into slime – maybe it's more of a girl thing. But sometimes it's excellent fun trying out the different recipes. If you add paint you can turn it different colours.

Nadia isn't like most girls. For a start, she doesn't care what she looks like. She wears shorts all year round, even when it's snowing. Mostly they are last year's tracksuit cut off at the knees. She doesn't care about brands either, or having a phone. But she cares about bees.

And fish.

And oceans.

And trees.

Nadia is big into scouts. She loves rock climbing and she's the best tree climber I know. She likes to hide up the beech tree by the gate and spy on us when we're out in the garden. It's pretty handy to have a sentinel over there if my brother chooses to escape by road. He mostly prefers the field, which is just as well 'cos the road is more dangerous and sets Mam into a fit of anxiety. If Nadia sees him making a break, she'll do her whistle signal to warn me so I can head him off before Mr Maloney's farmyard. It's a good system.

Nadia's older sister, Tanya, is BFFs with my sister, Kit. When they're together, they're the most annoying girls in the history of annoying girls. Tanya has long hair down to her backside, as bad as Rapunzel. Every time you see her she's brushing it. She would be absolutely thrilled if someone stuck her in a tower and visitors had to stand below, waiting for her hair to hang down in a ginormous plait. She would live there for ever, combing her hair until it fell out. She was mad to get the role of Rapunzel in the big school musical last month but one of the others beat her to it.

Kit was the horrible witchy stepmother. She was brilliant. I got to go both nights. The first time I missed the end because Joe did a runner from the lights. He hates when lights are too flashy or they use smoke or bangs or any of that crazy stuff. He bolted so fast, at first I couldn't see where he'd gone, but I'm quite an expert tracker now. I soon picked up his trail and stalked him to the Home Ec room, where he was raiding the place for snacks. He'd managed to make a substantial mess already. He's pretty expert at turning a place upside down in a matter of seconds. Mam says he has a gift for it. You can spend all afternoon hoovering the gaff, clearing away games or laundry, and in five seconds he'll have your room looking like a hay barn in a tornado. It's quite impressive, unless you're expecting visitors – getting the place presentable can be a bit of a stress in our house.

By the time I'd talked him out of there, I'd missed the end of the show. I could hear everyone clapping and cheering, so I brought him outside, where we wouldn't get mashed up in the crowds. Then we played chasing in the car park until everyone came out.

Kit was a great success at being wicked, so Mam took us all out for fish and chips afterwards. I love a celebration. Fish and chips are my absolute favourite.

Nadia gets very upset about fish in the ocean feeding plastic to their babies. They don't know it's plastic; the ocean is full of tiny floating bits that look like food. Nadia is on the case. She's the local recycling inspector. It's a bit embarrassing when she comes over to our place, as tidiness is not number one on the agenda. Nothing ever seems to end up in the right place. And things are always going missing. I could write a list of everything that goes missing in our house, but it would take a whole book, there's always something...

The car keys
The jam
Socks
School ties
Dad's glasses
The Sunday magazines
Drinks bottles
The butter
The sugar bowl
The Blu Tack

The Sellotape
Teaspoons
The remote controls
My mouth guard
Kit's exam notes
Her going-out tops, her best jeans
Her phone

Granny says, 'Say a prayer to Saint Anthony, and then search again.' It's her magic formula. Saint Anthony is the patron saint of lost things. The poor guy. He must be permanently searching for something in our place. He never gets a rest. If he took a holiday, we'd be screwed.

My brother is not picky about what he takes and where he leaves it. Last week the remote control turned up in the woodshed after two days. Kit's pencil case was found floating in a rainwater barrel. It's not like you can ask, *Where did I have it last? I'll retrace my steps.* There's no logic. It could be anywhere. You can see why Saint Anthony will never be out of a job.

You can't blame Joe for all of it. Mam says we're like a gang of elephants charging through the bush. I'm supposed to be in charge of recycling but sometimes I forget.

Housework is not my strong point. Sorting socks is the worst. Why do they come in different colours and with pictures on? Nightmare. The odd ones live in a bag together being odd. They probably love being odd. They're probably happy they lost the other stupid same-looking sock. Who wants to be the same? Who says the world is full of pairs, paired up into matching stripes. Our odd-sock bag is so big it's become a drawer. A whole drawer full of odd socks partying in there. Who am I to get in their way and spoil the fun? After all, no-one really notices if your socks don't match, do they?

Kit tries to keep her room locked so Joe can't get in to work his magic. This works well except when the key goes missing or I hide it during a fight. On the whole I try to avoid fights. I'm a man of peace – what can I say? Fighting with girls is the worst. What a racket. Kit has the worst scream. She sounds like a banshee dying.

Nadia doesn't say it but I know she thinks our house is kind of crazy. It doesn't stop her calling over, though. I reckon she spends more time in our kitchen than she does in her own.

Nadia collects facts the way Dad collects glue. They sit in her head in little drawers: tidy little rows of facts. She collects them from all over – from the radio, from YouTube, from nature books.

Facts about the environment:
Every ton of recycled paper saves seventeen trees

Facts about climate change:
Cutting down trees causes fifteen per cent of carbon emissions every year

Facts about plastic:
By 2050 there will be more plastic than fish in the ocean

Nadia cannot beat me at the two-kilometre park run. But she can beat me at facts. She can open that fact box in her mind and find one on any subject. She can flick through her files without blinking. She can open the drawer called rain and say, 'River levels are at an all-time low.'

'What do you think is more important?' Nadia asks
'Saving the Polar bears
or saving the bees?'
'Do we have to choose?
Can't we all pick different things, then everything will be saved?'

Nadia sniffs like her mother when you say something silly. She sniffs in Russian. 'We're destroying the planet,' she says. 'Even Saint Anthony cannot find the ice caps. They're melting away.'

Nadia thinks she can solve everything. Just because she's one month older than me, she thinks she can boss me around. I already have a big sister to boss me around, so when Nadia gets too bossy I tell her to get stuffed. But she's right about the ice caps,
and the Polar bears.
and the fish.

Once upon a time, Nadia's mother was a doctor in Belarus. Now she's a house-cleaner. She cleans dirt out of houses the same way she used to clean bugs out of bodies. It's basically the same thing, she says. But it pays better if you're a people-cleaner. Nadia's mum makes *machanka* and *draniki* for dinner. *Draniki* are potato cakes by another name. They taste delicious.

Belarus was a beautiful country until the whole place was poisoned by radiation. It was too poisonous to live in her town; everyone had to leave. You can go back now to visit. There are animals, even wolves, living in the empty houses. But Nadia's mum doesn't want to go back. She started coming here when she was a girl. They sent her away for the fresh air and clean water. Then she fell in love with an Irishman.

'It's a vairy romantic story. He was my one true love,' she says every time she tells it.

She blows kisses at his photo hanging over the stove. She talks to him as if he's right there, answering back.

But he's not. Nadia's dad died when she was only six. She moved here afterwards so I never met him, but in the photo he looks like a big bear. He has a grizzly beard and shiny blue eyes. If you look at him sideways it's like he's winking at you. I reckon he was one of the good guys.

TUESDAY

Eyebrows and Nails

I've started writing a new song called 'I Wish It Was School Holidays'. The chorus is pretty straightforward but I've only one verse finished so far:

Waking up each morning, my head is full of drool
The birds are singing but not in my bedroom
Gotta jump on my bike and ride two miles to school
Study all day, inside those walls of doom

Oh, I wish it was school holidays at last
Free to run around all day and play
Summer is here, I want to have a blast
Break down those walls and let us run away.

That's the chorus. I love the line about breaking down walls. All the best songs have a bit of action going on. I guess it needs a bit more work on the verses.

I need all the practice I can get because at the end of August I'm starting secondary. So things are only going to get worse. Everyone says it's going to be great, but the thing is, it's a huge school. There are over eight hundred kids in that school from all over the county.

In my primary school there's ninety kids and I know every one of their names. I could count them up for you, if you had the time. Most of them live on this side of town and I see them at sports and at scouts. Most of them have cousins in the school. Apart from Lucas – his dad is from Sudan and his mum is from Cork. And Kieran Brady, whose mum is Scottish – all his cousins are in Scotland. And Nadia. And me – I'm not related to anyone in the school. So not everyone, but, seriously, half the kids in my class are cousins with the other half. I'm not kidding.

Then we've to get a bus to secondary school. It drives half-way around the world to collect us, so I'll need to be out on the road waiting at ten past eight. Mental. In the winter it's still pitch black at that stage.

Having watched Kit for years falling out the door with her shoes half on, I'm not exactly thrilled by the idea. Kit has serious trouble getting out of bed. You wouldn't wake her with a chainsaw. And she's always missing something, which causes hell on earth until she's gone with a slam. Usually I wait till I hear that bang before I come out from under the duvet. And she takes forever in the bathroom.

Me, I just want to go and pee, get dressed, eat food. It's simple. Not Kit – she spends EASILY HALF AN HOUR doing things to her hair in front of the bathroom mirror. Not to mention her eyebrows. Eyebrows are the worst. I shouldn't even know this stuff. Lucas, he knows nothing about eyebrows. He has no idea you can pluck them or wax them or shape them like a wave. Why would I need to know that? I am never, ever going to need that information.

Unless I accidentally end up in a beauty exam – well, that would be funny.

> Question 1. Please draw a detailed map of
> a plucked eyebrow and make sure it is level
> with the other one.

Who needs to know this stuff? Like I said, all I want to do is use the loo. Half the time I end up outside peeing in the hedge, barefoot in the frost. I'm not joking. Dad says it will put hairs on my chest. I don't even want a hairy chest. I just want to use the loo in peace. Our house doesn't have a second bathroom. It probably needs five and it doesn't even have two. I would say this is the greatest cause of fights in the morning. If we had another bathroom it would be Happy Families, all of us showering and singing opera. But we don't. So that's another reason I'm not looking forward to this school.

Eight hundred kids is a lot of kids. Tommy K will be there and he's a creep. All the older guys who hang out smoking and giving funny looks when we're down at the shops will be there. Ray, who takes his dad's car and drives them all to the river, he'll be there. I bet none of them have ever had to deal with an eyebrow crisis at seven a.m.

They leave piles of empty cans along the river where we do our nature clean-ups with the scouts. You're not supposed to do that but no-one tells them what to do. Nadia has my head melted over rubbish in the river. It catches in the wings of the swans and they don't grow right. If it happens when they're young it means a funny wing for life. Irreversible.

Like with Joe. Some things you can change. And some things you can't.

So no, I'm not looking forward to this new school. Everyone else is fine about it but not me. Call me weird but that place looks like a prison – it's massive. I'll never be able to find my way around. You've got to do tons of subjects and exams as well! Kit was like a normal human being until exams came on the scene. And you get homework on the weekends.

So don't try to convince me it's going to be fun. You can't impress me with fancy words. If it looks rotten and smells rotten then it's rotten. I've heard the stories: some of those teachers are gremlins. If you get stuck with a bad one, you're screwed.

Lucas reckons it'll be fun. But Lucas doesn't have to deal with eyebrows. Lucas is super-good at maths and all the girls like him 'cos his smile takes up most of his face and he wears a leather jacket. He's got fuzzy black hair on his lip already. Next year he'll probably have a beard. Lucas doesn't even care but they're always joking about him being someone's boyfriend. Those girls have it all figured out. They draw pictures and write love letters from each other and leave them on his desk. Lucas couldn't care less. He just laughs. They never leave letters on *my* desk.

That's another thing about secondary school: they start on about boyfriends and girlfriends. Kit is the worst. She was great fun until all that started. Then it was all about this guy or that guy. None of them very nice guys. Now Nadia says its Tommy K she's into. I've never seen them together. Kit denies it. But she denies everything so that's no proof.

I'll punch him in the face if I see his ugly mug around here. Big shot. Who does he think he is? So he can hit a ball with a stick. Wow-wee. So he can run straight. What a champion! I heard what he said. She'd better not bring him over here. She'd better keep that loser at a distance. Nadia is probably making that up. She has an overactive imagination.

Blah blah boyfriends,
blah blah girlfriends.

It wrecks my head. Why do we have to get older and do that boring stuff? Can't we just hang out playing football and Minecraft, drawing cartoons and climbing trees? Why does everything have to get so serious? I never signed up for this. All this stuff in school about your body changing and growing hairier and the girls laughing their heads off when the teacher is talking about testicles. Hair is going to start sprouting all over the place and there's nothing I can do to stop it, unless I start plucking it like Kit's eyebrows. Man, that must be sore! I mean, do you actually pull the little hairs out one by one? Isn't that supposed to be a form of torture, not something you do for fun? Or maybe that's pulling out nails.

Don't even get me started on nails!
Talk about pointless.

Painting them, wearing fake ones. Tanya is the worst. I don't know how she even writes with those things on. On top of that, it's the end of the world if one of them breaks. I mean, seriously. A piece of plastic stuck to your finger?

Nadia hates those things. They probably turn up in the ocean with the plastic bags.

There's a green uniform in that secondary school as well. It's the worst. I hate uniforms – there's always something missing when I go to put it on. Mam reckons the tooth fairy runs off with my ties as well as my teeth. The tooth fairy! It's years since I lost any teeth. I'm too big for all that.

> Too big for Lego
> > and sandpits
> > > and rolling in the mud.

Growing up is so over-rated. I'm no good at clothes. As long as it covers me I'm not fussed. Joe never cares what I wear. Joe doesn't care what anyone wears. Forget clothes – he'd be happy to run around naked. When he meets people, he only looks at their faces, whether they're smiling at him or not. Whether they'll shake his hand or give him a smile. That's all he cares about. He doesn't know about plucked eyebrows or broken nails or matching outfits. None of it messes with his world. He won't have to wear a stupid uniform. Not ever in his life. He won't be bothered with lost ties or girlfriends or boyfriends. He won't worry if he fails exams or his hair looks funny.

It looks funny most of the time anyway.

Joe hates haircuts and it always sticks up at the back no matter how you brush it. Going to the hairdresser is Joe's idea of a sad day. You have to bribe him with sweets to even get him in the door. He can't sit still while they potter around taking bits off. A straightforward number three is always the best bet, apart from the time he ran out when it was only half-done. That was a bit of a disaster. That was a bad fashion moment for Joe. But he didn't care. He didn't even know. He never bothers with the mirror. Not like Kit and Tanya, who spend half their lives stuck to the thing. The walls of that school are probably painted with mirrors. Pathetic.

Until I was five I wore the same Spider-Man costume every day. In all our family photos, I look exactly the same except bigger: red and blue with a web face. Mam had to go out and buy a second one because I was heartbroken if it went in the wash. I can still remember how soft the fabric felt. I loved that suit. Getting dressed was so easy; all I had to do was get up and put the same thing on every day. I had Spider-Man pyjamas too.

I guess I had a bit of a thing for Spider-Man. I thought I was the best ever. I even thought I could fly until I nearly broke my arm jumping from the shed roof. Kit found me tangled up in the hedge. That was the worst day ever. If I had the choice of a superpower I would pick flying. When I was bored in school I could just fly out the window while no-one was looking. I could fly home and make a sandwich and lie in the garden instead of doing work. I could fly into town and buy myself an ice cream. I could fly away over a rainbow and be twelve for ever.

Tragedy. Tommy K, alias Gorilla Face, showed up this afternoon to coach us for our last week of training, laying it on thick. He loves playing the big shot. He made us all run laps of the pitch, just because we were having a laugh. Just because he could! It started when I went to get a drink. We'd been playing hard and I was roasting. The sweat was running down my back so I took my top off.

Then Lucas took his water bottle and squirted it down my front. I wasn't going to let him away with that; it was all-out warfare. Then everyone joined in and Kieran Brady got a bit over-excited. Kieran never knows when to stop. He's a bit like Joe that way. For some reason there was a bucket on the ground beside the rainwater barrel. Kieran filled it up to the brim and sloshed the whole lot over Lucas. He wasn't expecting that.

Things went downhill from there. It was mayhem. Tommy Gorilla Face K was spitting fire. He said we could all dry out in the sun and set us running laps. The sun was pelting down. We were clutching at each other's legs by the end, dragging each other across the pitch. Lucas lay on the grass and refused to get up. He thinks he's Ronaldo. He was waiting for a FIFA helicopter to land on the pitch and collect him.

Luckily I wasn't the only one with a stressful day, so we wound up at Peroni's for dinner. Our town has the best chipper in the world. Mr Peroni makes real chips from chopping spuds all day and he makes the best crispy batter ever. We are his as-often-as-it's-allowed regular customers so we always get a warm welcome. Mr Peroni has lived here since forever but he still talks like he's in Sicily. He always makes a fuss of my brother. Whenever we visit, he's on it straight away.

'Ah, Joey, Joey,' he says in his sing-song voice. 'Come in, come in!'

He introduces him to everyone and plays his favourite songs on the jukebox. He plays 'Me and Julio Down by the Schoolyard' and 'Hey Jude'. He never minds shaking hands thirty times. He doesn't give out to Joe for wandering around the place either, so Mam can chillax.

Other restaurants are not very tranquil with Joe. He doesn't understand that you can't grab food from someone else's plate. He's working on it, but desserts are a killer. He loves looking at everyone's delicious plates; you have to watch him like a hawk. Before you know it, his fingers will be wedged into some poor sucker's ice-cream sundae. So guess who gets to tail him around the joint as soon as he's gobbled up his food? At least it's good tactical practice for blocking the opposition. You've got to watch your back. And your sides. Eyes everywhere ideally. And I mean EVERYWHERE.

No room for slacking.

Mr Peroni always gives Joe extra chips and ice cream and makes such a fuss that he doesn't wander as much. It's a good business move too, as we hardly ever go anywhere else to eat and Mam always leaves a good tip. I don't mind avoiding the other restaurants 'cos fish and chips are up there in my top five. I'd eat them every day for dinner no problem. For dessert I like eye-ceem. That's one thing me and Joe agree on.

We were just about to cross the street back to the car, when Joe picked that exact moment to bend down and kiss the pavement. Now, apparently there are holy people who kiss the pavement. This is a fact. But in general you don't drop to the ground kissing the pavement at random spots. This is also a fact. Granny says he's like the pope getting off a plane. Try telling that to the people on the street. *Please excuse my brother the pope while he kisses the street. Make way for the pavement kisser.*

He doesn't even check it's clean. There could be chewing gum or dog poo or anything on there. Kit lost the plot. *What if one of my friends sees him?* she was thinking. I know that's what she was thinking. So she lands him a kick on the backside, which, you might say, is not very kind but I know she was freaking out.

'Get up, you nincompoop!' she said.

There was war at home because we're all trying to choose non-violent behaviour (along with acceptance). Non-violent behaviour is when you talk things out instead of belting someone. If you're feeling upset you take ten breaths before you act. Then you're more likely to say how you're feeling instead of freaking out. Or you might end up punching a cushion instead of someone's leg. Our fridge is covered in messages:

> *If you can be anything –*
> *Be kind*

> *Listening*
>> *Acceptance*
>>> *Respect*

>>>> *Negotiating differences*

Mam and Dad have been on a few hundred parenting courses. Our house is an experimental laboratory and we're the experiments, bubbling in our glass bottles. Kit has green steam coming out of hers. The thing is, you're wasting your time giving out to Joe. Half the time he doesn't understand what he's done wrong. I say *half the time* because the other half he's up to mischief. But it can be hard to tell the difference.

As you've probably gathered, our house is *not* one of those places where you're afraid to touch the furniture or talk too loud. It's more likely that no-one hears you unless you shout and the furniture is falling out the window. There's usually somebody staking out the kitchen, locking up the sugar bowl, almost always people arguing somewhere, loud music playing somewhere else and someone tailing my brother, because you never know what might be the next thing to catch his eye and be transported to oblivion.

WEDNESDAY

Sardines

Kit and her stupid exams. I'm fed up hearing about them. It's like a news report every day – which subject she's dreading the most, which questions will be her downfall.

Today on *Dreading the Exams…*
Kit talks about her chances of failing miserably and having no life.
We're all ears.

Tell me, Kit – how are you feeling about your next exam? Would you like to bore us for another hour with a long terrible story about writing the perfect essay?

I thought so. Please excuse me while I put my headphones on.

Talk about catastrophe! The whole place is on thin ice as a result. You can't fart without getting the evil eye. If a phone dares to ring it's disturbing her peace. (Unless it's her own phone. Funnily enough, that never bothers her.) If the football bounces off the window, she'll come rampaging over like a ferocious T-Rex. I'm a pretty chilled guy but there's only so much I can take.

We're all on our best behaviour. I'm supposed to tiptoe round the house and play the guitar extra soft. Talk about impossible! And what about poor Joe? He does his best but sometimes I think he gets more wound up the better he's supposed to be. Let's be honest, it's a lot of pressure for someone who can't even resist the sugar bowl.

And Kit leaves her notes all over the place. I mean *all over the place*. I was reading her biology book on the toilet yesterday because it was a choice between that and *Fine Woodworking*. So it's no wonder Joe made off with a handful of flash cards – how was he to know they were important? He can't even read.

The fallout:

Where are my notes?
I left them on the table –
I'm sure I did.
Maaaaaaaaaaaaaam, did you see my notes?

After twenty minutes of this, she accelerates into a full-blown meltdown.

Booooom!
Who took my effing notes?

(She starts throwing things around the place, which clearly won't help – it only makes a worse mess.)

Why won't any of you help me?
It's YOUR FAULT if I fail my exam.

YOUR fault.

ALL OF YOU.

(Nobody escapes the wrath of Kit.)

STOP LAUGHING at me!

(Fires a fork in my general direction. I duck.)

It's difficult to practise acceptance under these conditions. I usually try to tiptoe out of there before I get dragged in any deeper. Guaranteed I'll have done something wrong if I hang around, even if it's just the way I'm looking at her.

Stop LOOKING AT ME like that!!!!

What am I supposed to do? Close my eyes? Gouge them out with a stick? Grope my way blindfolded around the table?

Uh-oh. Footsteps thudding on the stairs. Dad's heading for the kitchen; this won't be pretty. Dad has a short fuse when it comes to meltdowns. The two of them will be *explosive.* I don't need to hear this. Get me out of here, quick!

But wait for it, a sudden intervention. Mam to the rescue! Here she comes, charging down the hall on her white stallion. She flings open the door and bravely enters the battle scene, chainmail glinting, white flag flying. I slip out while she's taming the dragon. It feels mean to desert Kit when she saves my ass so much, but when she loses it she really loses it. The best thing to do is get out until the explosion is over. Otherwise you're just another casualty.

So I was innocently lurking in the garden minding my own business when Joe appeared out of the hedge, clutching a stack of multi-coloured flash cards.

'No bold,' he said.

As if he knew exactly what was going on in the kitchen at that very moment. I noticed a trail of cards leading back under the hedge. Some of them were stamped into the mud. Even when I cleaned them up it was hard to hide the streaks of brown. I took Joe for a walk up to Mr Maloney's farmyard while Dad tried to discreetly return them. Poor Kit. Even though I laugh at her, I really want her to pass all her exams. I just wish she wouldn't blame us all. It's not our fault exams are horrible.

I'll still miss her when she's gone. She'll be leaving home in September to go and expand her brain cells in college. At least that's the plan. I don't know if it's real when she says she's going to fail or if she's just afraid. Sometimes I get scared before big matches, scared I'll make a mistake or do something stupid when everyone is watching. I guess she gets scared too. I wonder what it would be like on stage, playing a song for a crowd of people. I used to want to be a footballer when I was younger. I thought I was the best in the world. I'm pretty good. But I'm not Premier League material. I'm a strong hurler, but I don't know if I'll make the county team.

Mam worries what will happen to Joe when he's grown up. Even though he looks older, he doesn't act older. Not like the rest of us. Someone has to mind him all the time. She worries that some day he'll run away and we won't be able to catch him. Or he'll run out on the road and get hit by a car. There are any number of things you can worry about with Joe. Take your pick.

I was glad when Nadia turned up. Nadia is always hanging around outside, waiting for someone to suggest a game. She likes to pretend she's a camouflaged soldier hiding in the rhododendron bushes. She's always crawling around on her belly, rolling under the branches like a pro. She doesn't care if she's covered in brambles. Lucas hates brambles – he's afraid of scratches on his leather jacket. Nadia says he should leave it hanging up somewhere safe, but Lucas has never taken that jacket off since he got it for his birthday last year. I think he even wears it to bed.

'Fancy a game of Sardines?' she said.

'Sure.'

She knows Joe loves Sardines. He's awful at hiding and staying still but he loves the thrill of it. He gets super-excited and gives himself away every time. Dad joined us for a while, and when she heard us all squealing, even Kit came for the laugh. I love prowling around looking for everyone. Slowly the house starts to empty and you know everyone is disappearing but you're not sure where. I found them in the shower, squashed on top of each other, busting their guts laughing.

This evening, we had my end-of-school ceremony. Eight years of primary school and the principal wanted us to reflect on the highlights. I can't remember what happened last week, never mind five or six years ago. All I remember are the silly things:

The time Donal got locked in the store cupboard.

The day Nicola arrived with blue hair for our Paddy's day celebration because she got the colours mixed up.

When Lucas used to drive the teachers crazy with his fart noises.

The time we had a sub-teacher and everyone changed their names – Ríana and Sandra switched names but kept answering each other's questions and we were all in stitches laughing. That was a good day.

All the same, it was nice to walk up the room and get a photo and certificate to remind me of all those years sweating over 1 + 1 and ABC. I've got bigger fish to fry now. I've got to figure out this new school. All those corridors and weird subjects.

Mam was relieved that Joe was on his best behaviour. It's always a roll of the dice heading off together to an event. It can go either way. I could hear the other kids giggling a bit when Joe was walking up and down the back of the room. But they didn't mean it badly. They've seen enough of Joe over the years to be very understanding. And, I would say, almost unshockable. I bet they all remember the time Joe got to the Christmas Show snack table before anyone else. That was a disaster. I doubt that's on anyone's list of highlights.

After the ceremony there was tea and cake. Joe sat on one of the little chairs with a happy mound of buns stacked on his paper plate. He thought he had it made. If you play your cards right you can stuff yourself silly on toffee squares and rocky road while the grown-ups are yakking and catching up. This is the pay-off for best behaviour. The trouble is Joe doesn't have much of a long-term memory either, so you never know what's going to happen at the next event. But as Mam says, there's always hope!

THURSDAY

The Dark Side

I thought we'd be in celebration mode again tonight, now that Kit has *finally* completed her last exam. *No more drama*, I thought. *The end has come.*

WRONG, WRONG, WRONG! I can't believe my sister has gone over to the dark side. Nadia was right after all. I hate when she's right. Now I'll hear how right she was one hundred times a day until infinity. Tommy Gorilla Face K dropped Kit home this afternoon. They must have gone into town after she finished her exam. I'd never believe it if I hadn't seen it with my own eyes. Traitor. They sat down the road kissing in the car for a full half-hour before she finally emerged. I know because I was hiding in the hedge waiting for Nadia to find me.

I haven't spoken to Kit since. She hasn't even noticed she's getting the silent treatment. She's too busy whispering with Tanya and smooching at herself in the mirror. I want to pelt her over the head with a frying pan and say, 'Wake up, stupido.' Instead I'm trailing Joe around the garden and waiting for someone, anyone, to come get me away from here pronto.

Away from whispering, giggling girls

Away from Tommy Gorilla Face K bossing
everyone about

Away from Joe walking around and around talking
to himself

In the whole world of guys, why choose him? In the entire
universe of human beings, why does she have to pick the
hairiest, rudest, meanest person I know? It doesn't get any
worse. Kit never likes the good guys. Her last fella cycled
over my ankle with his new mountain bike and called me a
lightweight when I said it might be broken. It hurt like hell.
I'd a massive purple bruise that lasted for days. But even
he was OK compared to hairy monster man. Compared
to hairy, grunting gorilla man he was a dream choice, a
lucky star win, a top trump. I've got to do something before
she falls madly in love with this moron. I've got to save
her from his evil clutches before he crunches her up and
spits her out in chunks. I know what he's up to, the evil
mastermind. I need to come up with a plan that will send
him running in the opposite direction, never to return.

I might need to bring in reinforcements to help me with
this one. Even Nadia seems to think it's OK. How come
none of them can see through him? He has them all fooled
with his wide-mouth smile. Well, he doesn't fool me. Not
one bit. What if I rigged up a trap to catch him? A giant
rat-trap (for a giant rat). Or a huge pit he could fall into,
preferably full of venomous snakes. I don't know where

I'd get the snakes. I'm a bit short on vipers or alligators or poisonous spiders. Plenty of cow-pats, though – no shortage of green, gooey cow poo around here. Plenty of thorn bushes and acres of nettles. All I need is a giant catapult, a sling full of stinking cow poo. Then it's just a matter of aiming right. He won't be slinking back here again. He'll be too busy pulling blackthorn thorns out of his backside and wiping cow muck off his Adidas shorts. He won't mess with me again, that's for sure.

I need to find out when he's coming back, so I can be prepared. If I can get my hands on Kit's phone, I'll be able to see when he makes his next move. I'm all about strategy, me – it's one of the reasons I'm so good at playing chess. Lucas thinks chess is uncool but actually it's all about the plot. You've got to figure out the enemy's moves so you can be one step ahead.

For the moment, I'm strictly on observation. Kit changed her password after the last infraction – a long story I don't want to go into. As a result, I haven't been able to access any of their insidious plans. Plus she never leaves her phone lying around any more, not since Joe dropped the last one down the toilet in revenge. We all know that was no accident. You've got to pick your fights with Joe because you just never know what will come back at you. He's like an unpredictable boomerang that way.

On a positive note, at least this has given me some genius inspiration. I've started another song. It's got a super-catchy riff. I think this one could be big. I've been practising a lot. It's called 'Bad Boyfriend', and it goes like this:

Help, my sister is losing her mind
She's got a new boyfriend, worst of his kind
She thinks he's a perfect match
But I know he's a rotten catch

Help me, I can't stand this guy
Wanna punch him in the eye
Wanna knock him out for good
Tell me, don't you think I should?

He thinks he's the best in town
Walks about like he wears a crown
But really he's an ugly mole
I wish he'd fall down a deep dark hole

The only thing is, I feel bad for moles. I've nothing against them personally. I just needed something to rhyme with hole. Technically, he's more gorilla than mole with his massive hairy legs and muscles like tennis balls. But you can't be too picky when it comes to song-writing.

I love that line about the rotten catch. Now I need to figure out a chorus. It's hard to keep inventing lines. I wonder how rock stars keep coming up with new ideas? Originality takes work. And it's harder to practise 'cos Kit won't be happy when she hears this so I'm keeping it under wraps. I want to surprise her when it's finished. (If surprise is the right word.) I don't want anyone to hear it until it's done. So I hum the words to myself. I sound like I'm mumbling nonsense. This is the price you pay for creative genius. They can laugh now but some day they'll be begging me for tickets to one of my sold-out concerts. I can't wait.

Lucas and I hung out playing video games and I tried to plant the seeds for a gorilla hunt – my code for operation Tommy K. I need more operatives on this mission. But Lucas, he won't listen. He's obsessed with car chases. He's a total speed freak. He won't even play Minecraft any more. I love the way you can keep building for ever, expanding your empire of wacky structures. Not Lucas: he wants speed. He doesn't care if Tommy K is crushing on my sister with his primeval fists. Let's face it, the guy is basically a gorilla with a hurl. He hangs around the back of the Spar like it's his TERRITORY. If you get too close, he probably beats his chest and grunts. I wouldn't put that to the test, just in case. Who wants to know what happens when you come between a wild animal and their lair? I need to plan my operation carefully. The last thing I want is to wind up trampled into the ground by a pair of gigantic, smelly feet.

Lucas says Tommy K could be one of the team leaders for summer camp. Disaster. All the coaches love him. I don't want him bossing me around, telling me what to do. He can go train some other sucker – he's not training me. I'd rather be trained by a real gorilla. I'd rather run around grunting and beating my chest than listen to that loser. I'd rather swing from trees and eat bananas. You could do worse for two weeks of the summer. I love bananas. Lucas just doesn't get it. It's a waste of time trying to talk him round.

I let him race himself while I practised guitar. Joe came and played along. I don't mind when he strums too loud and makes a racket – I know he's happy to be doing the same thing as me. I sang him the new song; at least he won't spill the beans. He'd help me if he could. He understands. He can tell the mean ones straight off. He knows the ones who have a good heart.

After all –
It's not rocket science,

all you have to do –
is shake his hand

shake his hand
and say hello.

Who knew being angry could be so good for song-making? I'm on fire!
Check this out:

Help me, I can't stand this guy
I want to swat him like a fly.
If he comes creeping round our place
He'll get cow-pats in the face.

At dinner Kit announced she's going out to celebrate tonight. My antennae were up right away. I'm an under-cover spy on a mission. Then she openly mentioned his name. I nearly lost a meatball with the shock. This is getting worse and worse. I tried to bring it up with Mam when Kit was out of the room but that went all wrong. She's no idea what a fiendish creep we're dealing with here. Mam sees the best in everyone.

'Your sister needs her privacy; it's not your concern,' she said.

Arrrgh!

As if this doesn't concern me. It certainly does concern me. I am very concerned. And Joe would be concerned if he knew. If he'd heard how Tommy K was talking about him. If he saw the funny looks.

We should all be concerned,
one hundred per cent concerned

And not only that, we need to be acting on our concerns. We need to be coming up with a fool-proof plan of action. I seem to be the only one around here with any idea of how serious things could get. I'm in the middle of a crisis and all anyone can talk about is what to wear to the wedding!

What wedding?
The Italian wedding.
Oh, *that* wedding!

The Italian wedding, the wedding in Italy. Someone did mention it a while back when I was only half-listening.

I'd completely forgotten that Joe and I are staying home while everyone else is flying off to somewhere beautiful in Italy for some cousin's wedding.

ITALIA – home of pizza and ice cream, two of my absolute favourite things.

A wedding – one of my absolute least favourite things.

Which is why I said I'd rather stay in Granny's than wear

a smart shirt and do the whole wedding thing, even if it was in Italy. So shoot me – it was months ago when they brought it up. I'm no good at planning ahead.

Joe will be in respite. He would not be a good candidate for sitting quietly at a wedding. That would be his idea of hell. And I'll be in Granny's. I guess I didn't really think it through. No-one wants to be left behind either. It's too late to say anything now.

Mam is so excited. She hardly ever goes away. I don't see why I have to go to Granny's. I could survive just fine here by myself. I've got my bike. Why can't I hang out here with Lucas, eating my way through the freezer? Anything that's any good can be frozen: ice cream, potato waffles, sausages, burgers, more ice cream. You get the picture.

Then again, I know where Granny keeps her chocolate – in the top press where Joe can't reach. And I'll get to pick all the movies we watch. As long as I dig the spuds and wash them for dinner. And fix a few lights or whatever – she always has a list of jobs. The best thing about staying with Granny is there will always be dessert. Dinner is good but dessert is always cracking. I *adore* Granny's desserts…

Upside-down pie
Custard cream
Apple crumble
Swiss roll
What's not to love?

Much better than *The Great British Bake Off* because you actually get to eat the results instead of drooling at the screen. And she doesn't skimp on the sugar like Mam. She even makes homemade eye-ceem in the summer. You can't mention it around Joe or he goes ballistic. She grows raspberries in the garden and mushes them up for ice cream. I'm a huge fan. Granny's house still has the bunk beds that Dad used to sleep in; his car stickers are still plastered over the bedroom door. His box of toy soldiers and his marbles live on a shelf with some of his old books. It's like a museum to Dad.

It's weird to think that he was once twelve like me and slept in those beds with my uncle, Johnny. Uncle Johnny lives in Sydney now. He comes home sometimes around Christmas to take a break from the heat. We've never gone to visit. It's very pricey for all the tickets and it would be tricky for Joe on a long flight. He's not very good at tight spaces. Fields are more his thing. I don't think he could watch a movie all the way with headphones; he hates headphones poking in his ears.

But I'd love to go. Lucas went to Melbourne. He says everyone goes surfing at the beach all day. It's too hot to do anything else. It's so hot there have been terrible fires. Last year half the world was on fire as far as I could see. Lucky it's too wet where we live. We're more likely to be flooded out. A few years ago, the river burst its banks and some of the houses in town were flooded. But not us. We're too far away and uphill. So I guess we're safe for now.

Nadia says we'll all be burned up or washed away or mashed by earthquakes and tornados if we don't save the planet. It's a lot of pressure. I've been counting on her to sort something out but Nadia reckons it's a team effort and if everyone helps we can do it together. She's probably right about that. I know from experience that more than one person makes a big difference in a tricky situation.

But enough about the big wide world! Right now, it's a fashion show here in our house, with half-dressed women trailing up and down the landing in bits of lace. It's a competition to see who has the highest heels or who's most likely to trip and fall downstairs showing off their dress. Apparently weddings go on for days and you need tons of changes. Even Dad has the iron out. I knew there was a reason I decided to give it a miss. Watching them is enough to make my head spin. It's a double whammy for Kit, 'cos she's heading out tonight to celebrate the end of the exams. She's hardly visible in a whirlwind of fabric and hasn't even started on the nails or the eyebrows yet. But I know it's coming. Tanya arrived over twenty minutes ago with enough make-up to paint a shed.

I took off out of the house and went for a run with Nadia. We're training for the five-kilometre fun run. I came third last year. I reckon I could get the gold this year. Nadia's a bit slower than me but she's not far behind. We have a loop, around Mr Maloney's farm and down the Dark Road. It's only four kilometres but it's a start.

Nadia's mam made a stack of *draniki* for when we got back. So I didn't have to go home and watch the girls leave. Didn't have to watch Kit head out to meet her doom with that ogre. And Tanya was over at ours so I didn't have to listen to her dumb questions.

'Are they packed yet, Dan?'

'What's Kit wearing to the wedding, Dan?'

'How long are you staying at your granny's, Dan?'

'Who's Kit bringing to the debs, Dan?'

She's worse than a private investigator.

Nadia's house is always quiet, apart from Tanya. Sometimes her mum plays piano and you can hear it echo all over. She's really class. It sounds like a proper concert, like you've accidentally arrived at a show. I always feel like clapping when she gets to the end. It feels wrong to turn on the TV afterwards. Even when the music has stopped it's still there plinking in my ears.

Like when I'm cycling home and a song starts playing inside my head. I sometimes wonder where they come from, songs. Do you think them into being or do they just arrive in your head all ready to be sung? Nadia didn't mention Tommy K, so neither did I. I'm keeping my cards close to my chest. Strategising. No point in moving too soon. I could ruin it all.

FRIDAY

Hey Presto!

Trying to get everyone out of our house is like trying to turn an oil tanker in the ocean. I was up at the crack of dawn with Dad to drop Joe over to respite. Respite is at his school; they have some special rooms for the kids staying over. Brian was there to welcome him, so that was a definite plus. We checked out his room and unpacked his case. Joe didn't really take much notice because Brian had a bag with some new instruments. He said they could spend the morning in the sensory room working on some new sounds. Brian says all the right things.

> 'Let's go and play some tunes, Joe.'
> 'We're having sausages for lunch, Joe.'
> He knows he's on to a winner there.

Then it was back home, where I spent ages sitting sleepily on my rucksack in the hall while everyone ran about in chaos, throwing random questions at me.

> 'Dan, have you seen my…?'
> 'Dan, don't touch my…'
> 'Dan, can you help me find my…?'

Finally we all piled into the car and drove over to Granny's. I waved them off from Granny's front door. Then I walked over to school for my last ever day of primary school. It's only a ten-minute walk from Granny's. By the time I got there, I was ready to go back to bed. I thought I'd be so excited for the last day, but it felt a bit weird.

In no time at all I was walking back to Granny's on my own. Her house is so quiet. I wished there had been room for my guitar in the car. I was missing it already.

I've read all Granny's comic books. But if I don't find something to do, she'll be after me with a list of jobs. I don't want to spend my holidays doing jobs! I wonder how Joe is getting on? Joe will still have school in July because it's too hard for him to be at home all day. Mam says he is a full-time job. By that she means he is hard work because you have to watch him all the time.

In August he has summer camp. He loves summer camp. In another year I'll be old enough to volunteer. Kit and Tanya do it every year. Mam and her friends set it up.

'Everyone else gets summer camps,' she said. 'Why not them?'

Lots of those kids sit around at home all day watching TV. You can tell by the look of them: some of Joe's friends are so pale you can see your face in them. They eat nothing but chicken nuggets. And their families are knackered from minding them all the time.

For the camp, each child gets matched up with a volunteer teenager. That'll be me next year. It's a jam-packed schedule. They do swimming competitions and treasure hunts in the woods. Mam has it all figured out with her gang of women. 'The mammy mafia' Dad calls them. They meet at our house to hatch their plans. Always worth hanging around when they're due on the scene. They rock up with toffee cakes, Chocolate Hobnobs or at the very least chocolate rice cakes. (Chocolate-coated cardboard, Kit calls them, but better than nothing at all.)

Kit says it's super fun. I suppose it's like chasing Joe all the time except you've got a whole gang of kids. Not everyone wants to do a runner, though; everyone's different. Some kids are in wheelchairs so running away isn't an option.

At the end of the summer they throw a massive disco. I always go to those. Then you get to see the wheelchairs have an advantage, whizzing about the place like bumper cars.

Joe loves a good disco. He's mad for the cheesy songs – he's a big Abba fan. He watches *Mamma Mia* just for the songs. Well, it can't be the story because, let's face it, it's not exactly ground-breaking stuff, but Joe, he doesn't even really watch them singing. He walks around twisting his guitar in his hands, trying to sing along. I bet he would've been a singer if he were able.

Maybe if I head out to the garden and hang upside down from a tree, I'll get some ideas for my lyrics. It's worth a try. Hanging around in trees is one of my favourite activities. Last summer I started building a tree-house, but it never got finished. Dad doesn't want to put a ladder up in case Joe gets ideas and I sort of lost interest after wrestling with a pile of planks in the pouring rain while Lucas watched from the garden shed.

Lucas has a cool zipwire in his garden, but Dad won't put one up here in case Joe breaks his neck on it. He really hasn't mastered the art of hanging on to a rope; even with swings he's lethal. He just lets go in mid-air and acts surprised when he splats on the ground. Playgrounds are not as much fun as you'd imagine when you can't hang on or climb very well, but slides are always a winner. Joe has no fear when it comes to slides – he shoots down those things like a rocket, upside down and on his side – he doesn't care. He's a regular thrill-seeker.

'Bored? Pfff,' Granny said while pounding into a mound of dough. 'Use your initiative – there's plenty of old bikes out there in the shed.'

Well, she was right about that. Granny's shed is like a tomb to old bikes, most of them dating back to Egyptian times. I found one with two working tyres and brushed off the cobwebs to reveal a sad-looking faded orange banger that probably belonged to Granny when she was my age. The only helmet we could find was bright pink, with tiny daisies on. It's just as well I'm not too concerned about style. I hope I don't pass Lucas on the road. He'd never let me live this down.

It's only five miles from Granny's to our house but it took me ages on that bike. I was wobbling all over; it was like riding something from the Wild West. I passed Mike the Bike zooming into town. Mike the Bike is in Kit's class in school; he does triathlons on the weekends and Dad reckons he's our future hope for the Tour de France. Luckily he didn't recognise me.

Nadia was not so easily fooled. She was sitting on her garden wall reading a book when I cycled through the gate.

'Back already?' she said, without commenting on the bike or the helmet.

'Just picking up my guitar,' I told her.

'Don't forget your plectrum,' she said without taking her eyes off the page.

I hate how she does that. On the one hand, it's useful, because the trouble is half the time I do forget my plectrum and it drives me crazy when I don't have it. But on the other hand, it's none of her business if I forget it or not. That's the sort of thing I listen to every day following me out the door:

> 'Don't forget your school bag!'
> 'Did you pack your lunch?'
> 'Have you all your homework done?'
> 'Have you got a water bottle?'
> 'Remember to drink enough water.'

Remember to drink enough water! That's the stupidest thing I've ever heard. How could I forget to drink? It's not like I'm going to crawl home gasping: 'Help me, quick! I'm dying – I forgot to drink water.'

It's weird coming into your own house when no-one else is there. Like entering an abandoned ship. All the evidence of our messy lives but no-one there to prove we exist.

> A coat left hanging on a chair
> > A bowl of oranges tipped over on the table
> > > Dad's shoes lined up by the door

I poked around the kitchen and made myself a big fat sandwich. No point in leaving all that ham; they'll be stuffing themselves on pizza soon enough. I like being in the house when no-one's home. There was a bottle of Club Orange hidden at the back of the cupboard so I helped myself to that too.

Then I went upstairs.

Kit's room was open; she forgot to lock the door in all the rush. Her clothes were thrown all over her bed. Her books piled in a corner with the last of the flash cards, her spidery writing and sticky notes everywhere. She wanted to burn some of the books but Mam wouldn't let her. Said they were too valuable.

And then I saw it.

A glint of sun on the little screen.

Kit's phone, left charging on her bedside table!

Oh, she will be mad.

She's probably having an explosion in the car right now. Glad I'm not there to see it.

I bet she's yelling at Dad to turn the car around. But he won't do that. They were already late when they tore off down the road.

A fresh message just in.

From TK. We all know who that is, don't we?

Hav fun c u mon

What's he planning now? They do get back on Monday. Where will he see her?

I did the only sensible thing I could think of – I put the

phone and the charger in my bag. Then I turned my attention to the next obstacle. Kit can never remember her passcode – she's always locking herself out and changing it, so I knew she must have written it down somewhere, but where?

If I were Kit, where would I hide my passcode?

A careful search of her desk revealed nothing. But then I saw it, poking out from under her bed – one of those hardback sketchbooks, the kind she uses for a diary.

Hey presto!

The back page – a gold mine of passcodes cleverly disguised as phone numbers, but I can do this. I know which is which.

Who would have guessed that a simple trip to pick up a guitar would reveal such riches? I can't do anything too obvious or she'll kill me. They can't know it's me.

I just need to know what he's planning so I can stop this going any further.

Bang Bang!
A knock on the front door!

In a panic, I took the phone back out and stashed it under the bed before I stuck my head out the window. It was just Nadia.

'Make any interesting discoveries?' she asked.

'No.'

Freak-out. Can she see through walls? (Maybe she has X-ray vision; that would explain a lot.)

'D'you want to play a game or something?'

'I can't. I'm heading back to Granny's now.'

'OK.'

'She's making rolls.'

(She makes the best rolls. I love them when they're fresh out of the oven.)

'Where's Joe?' she asked

'In respite.'

'Does he like it there?'

'I guess so. He doesn't really say.'

Maybe if I tell her about the gorilla hunt, if I just tell her that I'm planning to foil Gorilla Face, she'll help me.

'You know that guy Tommy K – he was really mean about Joe.'

'He's kissing your sister.'

'I know.'

'I told you she liked him.'

'I know, you were right, Nadia, but –'

'He'll be playing for the county team.'

'Yeah, but –'

'He's going to ask her to the debs.'

'WHAT? How do you know that?'

'Tanya said so. She's usually right about these things.'

I hate Tanya. She's worse than the TV for bad news. She's always poking her nose into everyone else's business.

'He's a creep. I heard him talking about Joe. I heard him slagging him off. He's mean.'

I didn't mean to say all that; it just came out. Nadia turned her ear towards the window. I could see she was really listening. Her eyes were half-closed like when she's really concentrating.

'Oh, yeah?'

'Yeah.' I could feel the anger fizzing up when I said it. I could feel it bubbling in my stomach. 'I wrote a new song about it.'

'Can I hear it?'

'I guess so.'

'Why don't you open the door so I can come in? Kit won't like you being in her bedroom.'

Another thing she didn't need to tell me. I took the phone back out and hid it in my backpack before I went downstairs to open the door.

'Does it have many verses?'

'Three. So far.'

I got out the guitar and started tuning up.

'Your mum doesn't like him either,' she said, chewing on one of her fingernails.

'Doesn't like who?'

Nadia arched her eyebrows like her mother does when you ask a silly question. 'Who do you think – Spider-Man?' she joked. 'Your nemesis, of course – Mr TK.'

'Really? How do you know that?' I asked, surprised.

She didn't answer. She gave me that look again, eyes half-closed.

'She said nothing to me about him,' I said.

I didn't want to let on that Mam practically told me to mind my own business. None of my concern, she'd said.

Nadia tapped her fingers on her nose like she does when she's figuring out a problem.

'Play the song!' she said.

I gave it loads on the chorus. I reckon it's coming together nicely.

> She's got a baaad boyfriend
> A really baaad boyfriend
> But she won't listen to me
> No, she won't listen to me
> Baaad boyfriend ... baaad boyfriend ...

I think Nadia liked the song. She's the first person I've played it to apart from Joe, and he doesn't count because he likes all my songs. She sat there nodding her head when I finished, tapping her foot on the floor.

'I don't think your dad likes him either,' she said finally.

Dad? Really? How does she know these things? What is she – some kind of secret agent? I shouldn't have let her in the door.

'What's Dad got to do with this?' I asked. But she wouldn't say any more.

Then I remembered Granny's rolls and started packing up.

'I've got to run,' I told Nadia while I stuffed the guitar back in the case. 'Granny will be wondering what kept me.'

I never asked her about the mission to trap Gorilla Face. I certainly didn't tell her about the phone. I knew exactly what she'd say.

'Kit will kill you, Dan.'

'Don't do it, Dan.'

'Be careful, Dan.'

'Put it back, Dan.'

Sure I can tell myself that. Why do I need someone else saying it?

'Don't forget your plectrum,' she said, picking it up off the kitchen counter. I hate the way she does that. I was sure it was already in my back pocket. I locked up the house and found my bike. At least I had my own bike to cycle back on.

Granny's rolls were fresh out of the oven.

'What took you so long?' she asked, while I was breaking out the raspberry jam.

'That bike was dead slow,' I told her. No point in going into too much detail.

'I have a few jobs that need doing tomorrow,' Granny said. 'And shall we go and pay Joe a visit on Sunday? Maybe take him out for a few hours?'

My mouth was so full of soft roll and sweet raspberry jam that I could only nod my head as I made my way to the squashy green couch for the rest of the afternoon.

After dinner I unpacked all my gear and stretched out on the top bunk. I prefer the top one because I can look out the window. I plugged Kit's phone into the corner and turned off the sound. I don't want it bleeping and singing in here. No more messages from Gorilla Face, just a couple from Alisha, one of her lunatic friends. She must have her own crazy-head code; I couldn't understand a word.

I found TK listed in the contacts and stared at his name, daring myself to do something. I could call him up. I could say anything I wanted. But I mustn't let the power go to my head. She'd find out eventually. But only if they speak. I could break them up. I could tell him she's never coming back.

Hey TK I luv it here,
never coming home luv Kit

But he's bound to bump into her around town. I could try being honest:

You suck, Gorilla Face.

I could call him up and sing my song down the phone. I could send him a photo of Granny's garden flowers up close and pretend it's Italy. I could send him a photo of a dog poo.

I could get started on the jobs or Granny will have me working all day tomorrow. I think she saves up all her broken light bulbs for when I come to visit.

I wonder how Joe is doing without us? He hasn't been to respite in ages. There just aren't enough people to make it happen all the time. When he was younger he refused to go. He used to hate it there. I guess it depends who's on duty. Brian isn't there at night. It'll be one of the other staff, Elaine or Tina or the tall guy with the curly hair – I forget his name. I hope they remember he likes the light on going to sleep. Sometimes he likes his music on but sometimes it keeps him awake. We used to share a room till he was ten. I got really sick of things getting broken and lost all the time. Now that he has his own room I kind of miss him, until he's firing my Lego out the window. Then I want to kill him. Lucas has all his Lego models displayed on a big shelf; some of them have been there for years. *Star Wars* and spaceships, still looking exactly like when they were first made. That would never work in our house.

Granny asked me to put all the plants up out of the way. It's like distributing sandbags before the flood. I'd better not eat all of the rolls. Joe loves those fluffy rolls almost as much as he loves buns.

SATURDAY

The River

'Did you fix the light bulbs, Dan?'

'I did, Granny.'

'Did you clip the willow?'

'I did.'

'Did you fix the shed-door handle?'

'I did.'

'Did you empty the recycling?'

I knew I'd forgotten something.

I could smell the sausages cooking. No cornflakes here, it's porridge and sausages all the way. I'm not a big fan of porridge but when you throw in a handful of brown sugar or some apple sauce it's really not that bad. Especially when you know it's going to be followed by toast and sausages.

I could see where this was going. I reckoned she was adding to the list every time I finished a job.

'Can I make a few buns for later, Granny?'

Granny loves to see me baking; it always puts her in a good mood. And baking is my next favourite activity after guitar and sports. I'll never be on *MasterChef* but I'm pretty excellent at buns. I can make any type of bun for any occasion:

plain buns
choc-chip buns
gluten-free buns
lemon buns
butterfly buns
thick-butter-icing buns
– if it's buns you're after, I'm your man

I've a fail-safe recipe Granny taught me when I was eight. I've been using it ever since. You put everything in together and mix it up. You can't go wrong. Whenever there's a family occasion or school cake sale, Mam says, 'Dan will do a dozen buns,' without even asking. And I do. See for yourself how easy it is.

How to make one dozen buns in jig time (superfast):

1. Turn on the oven to 225°C.
2. Prepare your bun cases in a muffin tray.
3. Measure 8oz (240g) each of self-raising flour, butter and sugar into a bowl. Add 3 eggs on top.
4. Plug in the electric mixer. Start slowly and mix it all up until it's soft and fluffy, adding a drop of milk if it's too thick.
5. Using two spoons, scoop a generous spoon of mix into each bun case.
6. Bake for 10–12 minutes, until they are golden on top. Check them after 10 minutes by poking a knife into the middle and making sure no gooey

mix is left on it. If they are not quite done, give
them another minute or two. When the knife
comes out clean, the buns are ready.

7. Decorate in any way that you like. If you
   eat them while still warm they are especially
   scrumptious.

Joe loves buns. He hardly ever gets them so he goes mad
for them. Mostly he eats the top off and leaves the rest. It's
the toppings he's after. Last month I had a tray of buns ready
to go to the scouts' cake sale, and while I was opening the
car door he had three of them done for. He takes the head
off with one bite. A sad trail of bald buns left behind him.
He's so quick. Like a lightning rocket blast. He's the fastest
draw in the west when it comes to food. Even though it's
easier without him getting in the way, I kind of missed him
wrestling with me to lick the wooden spoon.

The buns rose nicely with beautiful golden tops. Granny
was delighted. I knew the timing was right for an adventure.

'I was thinking to cycle to the river. Lucas said he'd be
there this afternoon.'

'I suppose that's not a bad idea to keep you out of mischief.
Be sure to finish your jobs first.'

'I will.'

'And you'll be back in time for dinner?'

'I will.'

'I'm making a pie.'

'Great.'

'Did you do the recycling?'

'I'll do it now.'

'If you fill the boot of the car I'll drive over to the centre now – I've to bring the car to the mechanic's.'

It looked like no-one had done the recycling since I was last here. The shed was chockers with bottles and cardboard. After I'd filled the boot we had lunch. Usually lunch is just a sandwich but Granny had made a cauldron of carrot soup and we had buns to follow. I could hardly move by the time we were done. I heaved myself onto the bike and headed off to the river.

The sun was out. I had a warm breeze on my back all the way through town and out the other side to the river. The Saturday market was busy in the square. I saw Mr Maloney stacking his baskets of vegetables and the cheese lady unrolling her packages. I could smell the cheese all the way to the traffic lights. I went up on the pavement after the lights so I'd be safer going round the bend heading out of town.

If you take a right turn before the Black Swan, a skinny cycle path leads down to the riverbank. The path is overgrown with brambles. In August they'll be covered with fat, juicy blackberries. The riverbank slopes down to a wide cove. It's never really deep enough to swim properly, but it's perfect to cool down on a hot day with everyone splashing around. There's a rope hanging from a tree on the bank and we take turns jumping in off the rope.

Lucas wasn't there yet so I cycled down along the bank, watching out for him. I saw Ray pull up in his dad's red Hyundai with a few of the lads. The passenger door opened and Gorilla Face climbed out. They had a couple of plastic bags with them and one of those portable speakers. They set themselves up in the shade under a weeping willow. I could hear them laughing and shouting back there. Further down, there was a mum and a couple of barefoot kids playing with a bucket. She had spread a picnic blanket out on the grass and was reading a book while they played.

I wished Lucas would hurry up. I took a spin around the track and on the way back I saw him coming in the distance. Even in the hot sun he was wearing the leather jacket. He had a pair of those mirrored sunglasses on too. He looked like he was landing a jet on a runway, not cycling his old racer.

'Hey, Danzo,' he shouted, skidding to a stop. We left the bikes by the fence and strolled down to the bank. Lucas pulled out a big bag of lemon bonbons from his pocket and handed me a can of Coke. I felt bad I hadn't brought some buns or thought to stop at the shop. I was so mad to get the jobs done and get going, I wasn't thinking. One thing I can say about Lucas – he's always got something to share.

After we'd demolished the cans and most of the sweets we horsed around in the river in our shorts.

After a while Lucas said, 'I dare you to swing off the rope.'

I knew I'd get properly wet if I did that. But I didn't mind. I also knew Gorilla Face and the lads were up there sitting under the willow. The rope is tied to a long branch of a huge old sycamore on the edge of the riverbank, beside the willow. I wasn't sure I wanted to go near them, but I didn't want to say so. I hesitated.

'Go on,' Lucas said. 'Last one in is a rotten egg.'

So we walked up to the tree. At first they paid no attention. I grabbed the rope, swung out over the water – and dropped in with an almighty splash. It's the best feeling! I didn't care about getting wet – easy to dry off on the cycle home. But Lucas was still wearing the leather jacket. He dropped in twice and landed standing up so he didn't get it wet. I don't know how he managed that. After a while the guys started watching us. They were drinking cans of beer and throwing stones downriver. They started to cheer us on. But Gorilla Face wouldn't leave it at that; he kept trying to have a go at Lucas.

'Hey, Frizz,' he called. 'Frizzy Frizzhead!'

Lucas has this amazing mop of curly hair that sticks out around his head. He hates people laughing at it. For ages he just ignored him. But then Tommy K started in on the leather jacket and Ray joined in:

'Where are you going in the leather jacket, Frizzhead?'

'Who do you think you are, a rock star?'

'Will you sing us a song, rock-star boy?' TK started squealing like a pig playing air guitar.

'Did Mammy buy you the leather jacket for the confirmation?'

'He's Muslim,' said Tommy K. 'He probably didn't make his confirmation.'

'Funny lookin' Muslim,' said Ray. 'Where's his dress?'

Tommy K roared laughing. 'Yeah, where's your veil? I bet it won't fit on over his hair, Ray.'

They really thought they were hilarious.

'Shut up, guys,' I said.

They laughed even louder.

I looked around desperately but there was no-one there. The lady with the kids had packed up and gone. I could see Lucas was starting to get wound up.

'Poor lass, he doesn't want the leather jacket to get wet.'

'Stop it,' I said. 'Don't do that.' My voice came out all hoarse and squeaky.

Lucas's eyes were bulging out of his head. He didn't say a word but he went marching towards them up the bank. Tommy K waited till he was almost up; then he stuck out his foot and Lucas went sliding down into the soft mud by the edge of the river. His jacket was covered in sticky mud.

I climbed down and helped him up. There were streaks of slime running down his back onto his shorts. Lucas hates the muck. We took the jacket off and started splashing it clean. The good thing about leather is the dirt mostly comes off. We wiped it dry on the grass.

'I want to kill them,' Lucas said.

His shorts were manky.

'Me too,' I said, keeping hold of his arm so he couldn't go charging back. 'But I'm not sure it's a good idea. I don't want their blood on my hands. I don't want to be thinking up lame excuses when the gardaí come knocking on the door.'

He half-laughed, watching them angrily out of the corner of his eye. The guys were standing further down the river now with their backs to us, skimming stones and pretending we didn't exist.

'Look!' Lucas pointed behind a rock. Their bag of cans was sitting in the water wedged between the stones to keep them cool and stop them floating away. Lucas stepped carefully over to the bag. He bent down and looped his fingers around the plastic handles. He looked at me. I covered my eyes. I couldn't watch.

'Don't,' I whispered.

But I didn't really mean it. My heart was racing. He lifted the bag gently out of the river. The cans made a dull clunk but nothing more. Lucas started backing away towards the path. The bag was heavy. There were at least a dozen cans in there, held together by plastic rings. They dragged his arm down towards the grass, so he walked lopsided.

Any second now they could turn around and see him.

Any second now they would be after us.

Lucas backed carefully over the bank onto the path. Then he turned and started walking away faster and faster. I looked back beyond the willow tree. No-one was watching us; no-one had noticed. I turned and ran after him down the track. The plastic bag was starting to rip. When we reached the bikes, we knotted the handles of the bag and fastened it on to the back of my bike with a couple of bungees. Then we cycled like the clappers until we were back at the traffic lights.

Outside Hanley's newsagents there's a tall black litterbin. I stood in front of Lucas while he hoisted the bag of cans off the back of the bike and dropped them into the bin with a heavy thud. Only then did we stop and take a breath.

'I can't believe we just did that.' Lucas was doubled over laughing. 'The weight of them – me hand is killing me.' The plastic handle had made a red mark across the palm of his hand. 'I wish I could see their faces,' he said, cracking up, 'when they go for another nice cold beer!'

He high-fived me and picked up his bike.

'I told you he was a creep,' I said.

He nodded. 'Fair warning.' He grinned at me. 'I guess I figured it out myself.'

We walked the bikes across the road.

'Do you want to come over to mine?' he asked.

It was very tempting. But I knew if I went over to Lucas's big sitting room, we'd be on the PlayStation all evening and I'd forget all about the time and Granny would be waiting for me with her pie going cold.

'Not today,' I said. 'I'll come over next week when the lads are back from Italy.'

We cycled back through town together, as far as the roundabout. The strong heat was beginning to fade and a cool breeze fanned our faces as we zoomed down the main road.

Town was beginning to go quiet but the Café Bán had music playing out into the street and a bunch of people were sitting at tables outside, talking and laughing. I recognised one of the teachers from Joe's school. Mr Peroni was standing by the door of his restaurant, drinking a glass of lemonade; he makes it fresh every day. He waved at us as we whizzed by. The cottages at the roundabout had baskets of flowers on their windowsills – one after another after another. They were bursting with colour – purple, blue, orange, red and bright, bright yellow like an explosion of summer-time.

SUNDAY

The Bus

'Did you put the plants up high?'

'I did, Granny.'

'Did you empty the compost?'

'I did.'

'Did you dig the spuds for dinner?'

'Ahhh.'

'We'll have to take the bus over to see Joe,' Granny said. 'The car is in the mechanic's.'

'OK. I thought we were bringing him back here for a while?'

'Sure can't we bring him back on the bus?'

'I suppose we can.'

Though I didn't know if Granny had thought this out.

'The two o'clock bus stops at the end of the road,' she said

'Fine so.'

'You can go free with me. I have my pass. And Joe is free too so we don't need to be messing around with change.'

I guess she *had* thought it out. Except you have to be sixteen to go free on an old person's bus pass with them. I pointed this out to Granny.

'Stand up tall and don't open your mouth,' she said.

'Right.'

'And don't forget to dig the spuds before we go. They need to be washed as well.'

It was three hours till two o'clock. Did she have to keep reminding me?

'I won't forget.'

Kit's phone was hopping. Three more messages from Alisha but nothing from Gorilla Face. I wondered what happened when he went looking for a cold beer. He knows where I live. Except I'm safe at Granny's now.

It looked like Alisha was living it up. Her pics had lots of bare skin and people posing in bikinis. I felt bad she was sending so many messages and getting no reply. So I sent her a smiley face. Just one. It could easily have been an accident. The phone could have done it itself, sitting there charging by the bed in Kit's room. Which is where it still is, of course. Anything else is a mirage.

Alisha was big on the picture updates. There was a whole gang of them out there, wherever they were. Somewhere hot. With sun umbrellas and a pool. That really narrowed it down. I recognised a few of them. I thought one was her sister but the way she was kissing her in the last shot – that's not her sister. I know that girl from somewhere.

'What are you up to in there, Dan? I hope you're not staring at a screen all morning?'

'No, Granny. Just tidying up my socks.'

'Well, hurry up! It's nearly time to walk down for the bus.'

Nearly time. It was another half-hour before the bus

even left the station. We'd be waiting by the side of the road for ages. Granny is always early for everything. If she were in charge of the airport no plane would ever be late. She even arrives early to the cinema so you have to sit and watch the empty screen before the ads come on. I guess it's better than arriving late.

Which is what usually happens when it's me and Lucas. Last time we went we missed the first fifteen minutes because Lucas couldn't find his shoes. Then we spent the whole movie trying to figure out what had happened. I thought the good guy was the bad guy but he turned out to be the good guy after all. I don't know if we would've figured that out quicker if we hadn't missed the start or if it was meant to be a surprise all along. I still don't know what happened in those crucial moments. Unless it comes on Netflix I might never find out.

It was hot and dusty standing by the road. I wished I'd brought some sunglasses. After a while I felt like I was eating dust. I didn't remember a water bottle either. That's why going places with Mam is really ace. She has this tiny backpack. I mean, it looks tiny but no matter what you need she sticks her hand inside and it magically appears. There's always a bottle of water or something to eat or a pack of tissues or a penknife or a pile of string. I wish I'd put a water bottle in my backpack. I don't know what I did put in there. It feels kind of empty. I didn't really think about it too much. I was too busy looking at Alisha's new shots. I guessed they were drinking cocktails. The triangle-shaped glasses with tiny sun umbrellas?

When the bus pulled up, Granny pushed me up the steps. 'Grab that seat behind the driver,' she said, as if there was a rake of people coming after us. The bus was half-empty.

Granny waved her pass at the driver, who never even looked at me to see what age I was, then folded it back in her bag and closed it with a little snap. She held it tight on her lap and gave me the history of the townland while the bus sped along the road.

'That road down there leads to the big house,' she began. 'It belongs to some foreign lad now but it used to belong to the Fernses. They had a lot of land around here, until the uncle lost it all to gambling. He was a devil for the drink.' She tutted her mouth in disgust. 'He was a bad egg,' she said.

I nodded my head in agreement. It's best not to interrupt her when she's on a roll.

'And that house over there belongs to the Tierneys. The eldest son is in London now. Made a lot of money on the stock market. But I believe he lost most of it in the recession. Funny-looking lad – he had thick glasses that made his eyes look massive. He looked a bit like a grasshopper.' She paused to take a breath and consider his strange eyes. 'And that house over there, they had six daughters. One of them married an Indian man. From Calcutta. A big-shot businessman he was. They say the wedding was a sight to behold. But they were divorced just as quick. She's living in New York now.'

Most of Granny's stories end like this. I don't know why everyone seems to lose their money or end up divorced but Granny doesn't really go in for fairy-tale endings.

'And down that road is where your father used to work when he was a lad. It was an old milk-bottle factory. Of course, nobody uses them any more. The youngest daughter has it now. She makes bread. You know, the bread that people eat when they can't eat real bread.'

'Gluten-free?' I suggested.

'Yes, that old thing.' She rolled her eyes. 'There was none of that when I was a girl. You ate what was on your plate and you were glad to get it. We had to take the horse and cart if we needed to go to town,' she added. 'Sugar and flour, that was all we bought in the shops. We grew everything else.'

I've heard all these stories before, but it's still kind of amazing to think they didn't even have a car, and by the time I'm old enough to have a car, cars will be driving themselves.

'Tell me about the horse,' I said.

She smiled. She loves talking about the horse. 'The horse's name was Betty,' she replied. 'Betty was an old cart-horse – we had her from a foal. She did everything around the farm. Took the milk to the creamery, the piglets to the mart. It was my job to brush her down in the evening and give her a carrot when she was good. She loved a fat carrot, did Betty, or a crunchy apple from the orchard.'

'I wish we had a horse and cart.'

'There's a lot of work goes into minding animals,' she replied, looking out over the fields with her long-ago eyes. 'You wouldn't be lying in bed until nine o'clock with your heels curled up to your bottom.'

I suppose I wouldn't.

'Now, keep an eye out for our stop, Dan. We don't want to miss it.'

We got out at the crossroads and walked the half-mile down to Joe's school. There's a line of big oak trees growing along the road and they make a tunnel of green. The sun shone through in spots and pools. At the gate we buzzed the little intercom and Brian let us in.

'We're just signing Joe out for a few hours,' Granny said

'Oh, right, OK. Lorna didn't mention anything.'

'It'll do him good to get a bit of fresh air.'

Brian nodded and wrote his name into the book. 'Sign here, Mrs Keenan,' he said. 'Do you need any of his things?'

'Sure what would he need?' she asked. 'We'll bring him back after his dinner.'

'Right, perfect.'

He brought us down the corridor to one of the big sitting rooms. The TV was on. Joe was sitting in a chair fiddling with a tambourine, not watching TV, not seeing us arrive. Granny looked around, making her tut-tut noise – she doesn't believe in TV on a sunny day. Molly was sitting in her wheelchair watching *Matilda*. I love that movie.

'Hi, Molly.' I waved at her.

Molly can't speak very well but she always likes when you say hello. She did her sideways smile and lifted her hand.

'Now, Joe,' said Granny in her we-mean-business voice, 'hop up there. We're going to take you out for a walk.'

Joe kept fiddling with the tambourine.

I took his hand and looked in his eyes. 'Come with us, Joe,' I said quietly. He doesn't like when people shout.

He stood up, still playing with the tambourine.

'We need to leave that here,' I said. 'You can have it when you get back.'

I thought he was going to make a fuss, but he dropped it on the chair and made a run for the door. Then we were off. I let him run all the way to the gate, but then I had to hold his arm and try to keep up with him.

'Slow down, Dan,' Granny called. But there's no slowing down with Joe.

'I'll wait for you at the cross,' I shouted, and we ran on down the road.

'You're like a pair of young foals the two of you,' she said, when she arrived panting at the cross. 'I can't keep up with you at all.'

There's a small shop on the other side of the road and Joe was going ballistic because he knows they sell cones.

'Eye-ceem,' he insisted, dragging me over.

'We're waiting for the bus, Joe,' I said. 'Not now.'

He's getting so strong, it was hard to stop him pulling me onto the road.

'What does he want, Dan?' Granny asked.

'Ice cream,' I said. 'He knows they sell ninety-nines across the road.'

'Sure can't he have one,' she said, 'if it'll make him happy?'

I had this funny feeling it wasn't a good idea but I couldn't think of a reason why. Joe was pulling on my arm. Granny handed me a fiver.

'Be quick,' she said. 'The bus will be passing now soon.'

We dashed across the road to Mrs Anderson. Mrs Anderson

has a tiny little shop with a faded blue sign over the door. She sells cones, sweets, biscuits, the papers and piles of logs for the fire, which she keeps stacked up outside the door.

'Well, good afternoon, Dan and Joe,' she said. 'What'll it be today?'

'Two ninety-nines, please,' I said. 'I'll pay first.'

And I handed her the fiver so my hands would be free for the two cones. I wasn't about to pass up the chance of a creamy mound of ice cream.

'A lovely sunny day it is today,' said Mrs Anderson, wiping her hands on her white apron.

'It is,' I said.

I didn't want to be rude but I didn't want to get her talking either. Dad says Mrs Anderson would talk the hind legs off a donkey.

I glanced out the window. There was no sign of the bus. Granny waved from across the road.

'I mind the day your dad cycled out here looking for that lost wee pup. It was a lovely sunny day, just like today.'

I've heard this story a million times.

'He can't have been much older than you are now.'

He was ten.

She held the cone under the nozzle and twisted it slowly, letting the ice cream unfurl in a perfect swirl.

'He was such a handsome wee fella, with his curly locks. Och aye, a handsome wee fella.'

'We're waiting on the bus,' I said.

She carefully placed the Flake in the side and reached for the syrup.

'Will it be raspberry or lime today, sir?' she asked, smiling at Joe.

Joe is never more patient than when he's waiting for ice cream. He is your dream customer, as long as you keep swirling.

'He'll have raspberry,' I said.

She handed me the cone and started on the second one.

'Cone, cone,' Joe said, trying to reach it out of my hand. 'Eye-ceem.'

'Just a minute, Joe.'

I wanted to wait until I had mine, so he didn't demolish his own one before I'd even started. Mrs Anderson watched us with one eye and made the second one quicker.

'Good lad,' she said as she handed it over the counter into my other hand.

I couldn't keep it back any longer. Joe had the top swirl eaten off before we were even out the door. We crossed the road back to Granny just as the bus appeared over the crest of the hill.

'Perfect timing,' she said and stuck out her arm to alert the driver.

It was only when we were going up the steps of the bus that I noticed Joe had bitten off the bottom of the cone. The bus was more crowded this time. There was only one set of seats left up the front so Granny sat in beside Joe and I was standing beside them. Ice cream started dripping everywhere – he couldn't lick it up in time. Granny hates a mess. She started shuffling around in her seat looking for tissues, but of course we didn't have any. It was leaking onto the seat and the lady across the way started giving us filthy looks.

I handed Granny my cone and I tried to take Joe's back so I could lick it into shape – 'tidy it up', Dad calls it. But Joe didn't want me to take it so he pulled it back and somehow it did this weird flip and a fat blob of ice cream went sailing back through the gap between the seats.

'What the...?'

I looked over the headrest. There was a man sitting there with a short spiky haircut, a skinny moustache and a splat of ice cream in one eye.

'I'm so sorry,' I said. 'We don't have any tissues.' It came out in a squeaky voice.

He stood up angrily, fumbling in his pocket for a tissue. 'What's going on?' he asked.

Granny was wrestling with Joe. He'd noticed she was holding my cone and he was going in for the kill.

'No, Joe.' I tried to grab it back. But just then the bus went over a bump and I lurched to the side.

And so did my ninety-nine.

Straight into the lap of the lady across the way.

'I'm so sorry,' I wailed.

I tried to lift it off her skirt, where it sat like a perfect sandcastle soaking into her lap.

Joe made a grab for it across the aisle and put half of it into his mouth. The bus swerved and it dribbled down his face. The woman watched him, horrified, but she was so mad, no sound was coming out. Yet.

The bus driver was looking at us in his mirror. 'What's going on back there?'

'He didn't mean to cause a fuss.' Granny was arguing with the man with the spiky hair.

'Sit down, please,' the driver grumped.

The lady opposite was red with annoyance. 'Carrying on like animals,' she muttered angrily, pulling a packet of tissues from her handbag.

I really wanted to ask her for some. I desperately wanted to grab one. It was everywhere, a river of sticky ice cream and melted Flake. Then Joe leapt up out of his seat like a rocket.

'Toi-let,' he mumbled, polishing off the last of my cone.

Great. Just great.

'He needs the toilet,' I told Granny.

'Sit down, Dan,' she said, clearly exasperated by all the action. 'We'll be there in twenty minutes.'

'He can't wait twenty minutes, Granny. He can't hold it after eating ice cream.'

This was starting to feel like a downhill adventure. I helped him out into the passage between the seats and we stumbled down to the end of the bus. There was a sign on the toilet door: *Out of Order.*

'It's out of order, love,' said a smiling face from the back seat.

She reminded me of Mam. At least she was smiling at us.

'I can see that. He needs to go now, though.'

I tugged at the door. I should have thought about the ice cream. It always makes him want to go to the loo. I should have remembered. I felt like beating down the door.

Joe pulled at the handle. 'Toi-let,' he said again.

I knew we didn't have much time. I whammed the door with my fist. Whimpered. The other passengers stared out the window; the children stared at Joe. I wished they would stop looking and do something.

The lady in the back seat spoke again. 'Ask the driver to stop,' she said.

'What?'

'Rogan's Garage, coming up now in a couple of minutes. He'll let you out.'

I knew she was right; it was the only solution. I pushed Joe up the bus, shouting to Granny on the way.

'You've got to let us out,' I said to the driver.

He rolled his eyes. 'What in God's name –' he started.

'Please let us out at the garage – look, it's just ahead.'

I could see the red sign appearing on the horizon like an oasis in the desert.

'I can't do that. That's an unauthorised stop.'

I didn't know what to say to that. Clearly this guy didn't get it. I pushed my eyebrows up into my forehead like Nadia and gave him *the look*. 'Well, you'll have some unauthorised stink on this bus if you don't let us out,' I said in the end.

He grunted and shook his head, muttering crossly, 'All right, all right.'

The bus started slowing down.

I pulled Joe down the steps.

'Toilet,' I said, as we tore past the petrol pumps. I stuck my head in the door; there was a lanky long-haired guy behind the till.

'Toilet?' I said, panting with exhaustion.

He pointed round the back, behind the car wash.

The door was open.

We were in.

I'd never felt so glad to see a toilet and a sink. We must have been twenty minutes in there. I could have lived in there for ever. There was everything, loo roll, paper towels, water, soap.

Granny was sitting on a bench by the car wash when we came out. She didn't mention the bus, the ice cream, nothing.

'You took your time,' she said, looking at her watch. 'The next bus won't stop here; it's not an authorised stop. And I was planning to get a tray bake in the oven.'

I didn't know what to say to that. Frankly, I didn't really care about tray bakes or anything else. All I cared about was that we'd managed to avoid the *toilet in the trousers* situation. That was close. I was so relieved I could have lain down and taken a nap by the side of the road. Granny took out her purse and started fixing her lipstick.

'Do you have a phone with you?' she asked.

'I'm not allowed a phone,' I said. 'Not until I'm in secondary school.'

It's not so far away now. August, September, whenever. And the only possible silver lining – my own phone.

'Don't you have yours?' I asked.

'I left it at home,' she said. 'I was using the timer for the sausages.'

Granny is always forgetting her phone.

Joe was getting restless on the bench.

'Maybe we can hitch a ride,' I suggested.

I looked up and down the road. The sun was splitting the stones and there wasn't a car in sight.

'When does the next bus come?' I wondered out loud.

'I told you he won't stop.' Granny was starting to get ratty. She put away her lipstick and snapped her purse with a sigh.

I looked inside where the long-haired guy was reading *The Local Guardian* and munching his way through a giant bag of crisps. Some people have it easy. 'Maybe we can ask yer man to call us a taxi.'

'A taxi?' said Granny. As if I had just said 'an elephant'.

We didn't get a chance to finish that conversation because just then a blue Nissan Micra pulled in beside the pumps and stopped with a screech. I recognised it right away – Mrs Turner's son, Philip, from the top of our road.

'Hey there, Dan,' he said, strolling over. 'What's the story, morning glory?'

Philip dropped us all back to Granny's.

'It's no bother, Mrs Keenan,' he insisted, piling everyone in.

I clipped Joe's seat belt and tried not to let his dirty clothes mark the back seats. Philip's car is completely spotless inside, as if it's brand new. No-one throws crisp wrappers or apple cores or melts ice cream in the back seat.

'When are your parents coming back, Dan?' he asked, flicking through the radio for Lyric FM.

Piano music started playing and Granny relaxed in her seat. I recognised the tune from Nadia's mum.

'Monday,' I said.

Tomorrow. It felt like light years away. I was already thinking about the bus back. Getting Joe back to respite.

I was beginning to think maybe we should ... Then we were at Granny's house and climbing out of the car.

'I'll turn the oven on,' Granny said as soon as we were in the door.

Then I remembered the blasted spuds. I forgot to dig the spuds. I took the shovel and went out the back with a bucket. I was only out there a couple of minutes when I heard Granny shout. What now? I tore back inside and, sure enough, Joe had already upended one of the plants in the hallway. It took one of the framed photos with it on the way down and the glass was smashed into a thousand tiny pieces. It was the photo of Dad on his wedding day.

I took Joe to the sitting room and tried to find some music on my iPad. There was nothing there for him to do. If I gave him my guitar he could break it. I wished the others weren't away in Italy. Why did I even agree to this? Joe always gets bored hanging out in Granny's. Whose big idea was this?

I took him outside to help me dig the spuds. *If I can just keep him quiet until dinnertime*, I reasoned, *we'll be taking him back straight after. And it won't be the same on the bus. There'll be no ice cream. And hopefully a different driver.*

The tray bake was delicious. It was a chicken one that Granny often does. Joe ate three helpings. And we had sponge cake for dessert.

After we cleared up, Granny got out the bus timetable and broke the bad news.

'That's odd,' she said. 'I was sure there was another bus at six-thirty but it says here there's nothing until ten.'

'Ten is too late,' I said, my heart sinking.

'I know that,' she replied, turning the timetable over in her hands. 'I'd forgotten, today is the Sunday timetable.'

Well, that was just great.

'He can sleep in the bottom bunk with you,' she said. 'A sleepover.' As if she'd just come up with a genius idea. 'I'll ring the school and explain. We'll drop him back tomorrow. The car might be ready by then too.'

By this time I was flaked out on the couch and Joe was sitting still for the first time all day. I was happy enough not to have to deal with the bus.

'He doesn't have any pyjamas,' I remembered.

'Can't he wear something of yours?' she said.

So at eight-thirty I got Joe sorted with one of my T-shirts and tucked him up in the bottom bunk.

'Is there any key for the door?' I asked Granny.

'For what?' she replied. 'Sure won't you be in there with him?'

And she shuffled back down the hallway as though that was that.

I didn't want to worry her, but I was thinking of the bedtime routine at home:

> The sugar bowl and the jam carefully hidden up high…
> The windows closed…
> The doors locked….
> The music for the morning…
> And the binoculars upstairs.
> *What if he goes wandering?*

Then Kit's phone lit up, silently vibrating.

TK.

The man himself, that moron!

What does he *want?* I wondered, looking at the phone.

I picked it up. It was so tempting to slide the little lock across. Maybe he'll leave a voice message. Kit never listens to her messages. Mam said she left her fifty messages one week and she didn't listen to any of them. I'm not surprised. Fifty messages!

It stopped.

I waited for a message but nothing came.

'Did Joe brush his teeth, Dan?'

'He did.' Eventually. Total nightmare trying to get Joe to brush his teeth. He couldn't care less about cavities.

'Did you brush yours?'

'I did.'

Joe got back out of bed and started heading down the hallway. I trailed after him, pleading with him to get back into bed. He poked around the kitchen for a while, opening Granny's cupboards. I followed him, picking up and putting back so Granny wouldn't freak out about the mess.

Finally he followed me back to the room. I got the guitar out and played him a few tunes. He loves the classics. 'Hey Jude', 'I Wanna Hold Your Hand' – I made my way through the full repertoire. Then I played the new song. It gets catchier every time I play it. No wonder Nadia was tapping her feet. I sang it a few times round and round.

Help, my sister is losing her mind
She's got a new boyfriend, worst of his kind
She thinks he's a perfect match
But I know he's a rotten catch.

Finally I could hear Joe snoring down below.

The phone lit up again. Alisha and the gang still giving it loads. I don't think Mam would like to see those pics. Definitely not PG. I took my time flicking through them – girls dancing on the beach at sunset, Alisha and the other girl (what's her name again?) lying in the sand. Some guys would love this stuff.

But I've got more important fish to fry. I lay in bed racking my brain for genius ways to trap Gorilla Face.

MONDAY

'Tips'

Before I knew it, it was morning time. I opened my eyes and remembered the day before. I rolled over and stuck my head down under my bunk.

No-one there.

I should have known. I slid down out of the bed, dragging the duvet after me. I was still waking up as I stumbled into the kitchen, wondering what the heck he was doing this time. The fridge door was wide open, making a beeping sound. A pool of milk was spreading across the floor like a white lake. He'd located the sugar bowl. It was tipped all over the table. And the raspberry jam. He was eating it out of the jar with his fingers.

'No bold,' he said, without looking up.

'Leave some for the rest of us, Joe.'

I took the jam and spread some on a roll for him. He was covered in jam. It was all over his hands and face, even stuck to his hair. I don't know how he managed to get it in his hair. I got a cloth and started to clean up the milk.

Granny came in the back door with an armload of salad and a bucket of green beans. 'Ah, you're up, boys.' Followed by, 'Merciful mother of God, what are you doing with the jam, Joe?

'I put his clothes in the wash,' she confided. 'They were *filthy. Filthy altogether*,' she added for good measure.

'What's he supposed to wear now?'

'Can't he wear something of yours?' she asked, making up a pot of porridge.

In theory, yes, but I hadn't exactly planned for this eventuality.

'Well, you've clearly helped yourself to breakfast,' she said, wagging a finger at Joe.

'Dam, dam,' he said, licking his fingers.

There was half a jar on there. At least it kept him busy for a while. He was really concentrating as he licked every tiny bit. Granny served up porridge and put some sausages under the grill. There was apple sauce for the porridge.

'*Now* where's he got to?' Granny muttered, putting her spoon down.

I looked up. Joe's chair was empty. I tell you, superpowers like you have never seen! He's like a disappearing act. You think he's there beside you, licking jam, then suddenly you look up and he's vanished into thin air. The back door was ajar. I looked out the window and I could just see my *Star Wars* T-shirt disappearing into the hedge.

'I'll get him,' I said. 'He's just at the bottom of the garden.'

'Good lad,' she said. 'Remember, that's an electric fence on the field next door.'

The electric fence. Crap.

'Joe,' I called, running down the garden.

I never know whether it's best to call or not. If he's really in the mood for a chase it can just make things worse.

But I was thinking of the electric fence.

Anyway, I needn't have worried because he got himself caught in the barbed wire on this side of the field. And ripped a massive hole in my best T-shirt. But at least he was there, impaled on the fence. I untangled the shirt and brought him back to the house while Granny called encouragement from the window.

Granny got a facecloth and tried to get all the jam off. 'How did you manage to get it in your ears?' she scolded.

'No bold,' he said.

'I think I smell something burning,' I said, sniffing the air.

'THE SAUSAGES!' Granny howled and grabbed the oven mitts.

They were totally black on one side. Cindered.

I was gutted about the sausages. They were inedible, really, but we saved a few bits of the less charred ones. Then Joe scoffed my share while I wasn't looking. At least I think it was him. (Unless there's some other invisible sausage-eater hiding under the table.) No point in being mad. 'You snooze you lose.' That's what Kit says. But it's easier when there are more of us to keep watch.

Then we got dressed. Even though he never stops eating, Joe is as thin as a rake from running everywhere, and I've grown a lot the past year. He looked like a scarecrow in my shorts. Joe doesn't give a hoot what he wears, but Mam hates him looking a mess. She gets me and Kit to do his clothes shopping. She always has him looking really smart – most of his clothes are smarter than mine, at least until he drags them through the fields.

The shorts were way too loose; they kept falling down. Joe just ignored them and walked around with them hanging off his backside. He was walking around the garden playing with a piece of stick, still in my T-shirt with the massive rip on the front. I wasn't keen to part with another one. How does Mam manage it? How does she keep track? I started to make a mental list of what we needed to do:

> Don't take my eyes off him for a minute
> Get him some clean clothes
> Bring tissues everywhere
> Get him back to respite
> No food before the drive

I can see why Mam has her lists everywhere.

'When will the car be coming back from the mechanic's?' I asked.

'I'll walk down there now and find out,' Granny said. 'You keep a good eye on your brother. I'll be back shortly.'

'Right.'

I locked all the doors and got out the guitar. I'm reworking the school holidays song. I reckon it needs some extra zing. There's something up with the rhythm. And I wanted to write some more verses. Joe listened for a while but he was missing his guitar; he kept trying to grab mine. So I let him play it for a bit. I thought I remembered seeing an old tambourine in one of the boxes in Dad's old bedroom. So I went to look for it.

Kit's phone was hopping. It was all go with the lunatic fringe out foreign. Three of them were messaging her now. Enough photos to poster a wall. More cocktails. More bikinis. Those girls were having a *blast*. Nothing from TK – or was there? A-ha, bingo!

Outside Peroni's at 1?

Here we go!

I sent him a thumbs-up. Then deleted the messages. Now I knew where I had to be at one o'clock, or where she was not to be. If only I had a cannon that could be packed with cow-pats.

But first we needed to get Joe back to school. I hunted around for the tambourine and eventually found it under a mound of old car magazines. I knew I'd seen one. 'Joe – look what I have!'

No answer.

'Joe?'

> Not in the sitting room
> Not in the bathroom
> Not in the kitchen
> Where is he?

I was tearing out the back door when I heard the doorbell jangling. I raced back to open the front door. I was in such a state worrying over Joe that I tripped over the umbrellas in the hall and landed with a mighty thud on the welcome mat. I dragged myself up and opened the door.

Granny's neighbour Patsy was standing there with Joe, his shorts practically around his ankles.

'I found this fella heading out the garden gate,' she said. 'I was just trimming the roses.' She waved the secateurs at me.

'Thanks a million, Patsy,' I said. I was trying to stand up straight, but my leg was battered by the umbrellas. 'He must have climbed out the window.'

She gave me a funny look and tried to look around me, into the house. 'Is your granny there?' she asked.

'She's just gone over to the mechanic's to see if the car is ready. So we can take Joe back to school.'

'I see.'

I could tell she didn't know whether to leave him with me or not.

'I'll keep a better eye on him,' I said. 'I won't let him out again. Come on, Joe.'

'Dam?' he said hopefully, stepping in the door.

'You've eaten all the jam,' I replied.

'Eye-ceem,' he said.

'Not today, and you're not allowed to climb out Granny's window either.'

'No bold,' he said and made a beeline for the kitchen.

I limped down the hall after him. That's the trouble with having a superhero brother. It can be hard to keep up sometimes.

A few minutes later, I heard the crunch of car tyres pulling up on the gravel outside. I hoped Patsy was already gone, but of course she was still lurking about spying on us. I could hear voices murmuring in the porch.

'Well, I can't leave you for a minute,' Granny said, coming in the door.

'I didn't expect him to go out the window,' I mumbled. She didn't know what to say to that.

She pursed her lips and looked over at Joe, who was rifling through one of the cupboards, upending jars as he went.

'Let's get you back to school,' she said with a sigh. 'We'll drive over by home on the way – you can grab him a change of shorts. We want him looking right arriving back. We wouldn't want them to think we couldn't manage.'

She looked at me knowingly.

'No, we wouldn't,' I agreed.

'We won't say anything about Patsy,' Granny added.

'No.'

'Or the bus.'

'No.'

'Or the sausages.'

The sausages! No-one cares about the sausages. But Granny does. She never burns ANYTHING.

'No, we won't say anything about them either.'

She sighed. 'Get your bag,' she said. 'And don't take your eyes off your brother.'

This time I was on the alert. I packed some wipes, a water bottle, some snack bars, a penknife and a pile of other random things. At the last minute I put Kit's phone and her charger into the bag. Now that I had time, I was wondering if I should leave it back at our house. Granny started the car and we headed off.

'No gool,' Joe said.

'What's that?' Granny asked, watching us in the mirror as she pulled out of the drive.

'He said, "No school."'

'Poor auld pet,' Granny muttered. She turned the car onto the main road.

We pulled up at our house a few minutes later. I got the spare key from the shed and we all trooped in. Granny took one look at the kitchen and started tidying up the counters.

'They won't want to be coming back to a mess like this,' she said.

I took Joe upstairs to look for some clean clothes.

'No gool,' he said, following me up the stairs.

'It's only until tomorrow,' I explained. 'Mam will collect you tomorrow after school.'

'Moro,' he repeated.

There was nothing in any of Joe's drawers. I don't know what he does with his clothes. Kit stacks them up in neat piles but there's never anything there when you go looking. I went back downstairs to search the laundry basket, but it was overflowing with girls' knickers. As always.

Granny was going for it in the kitchen. Dishcloths were flying. There was a visible mist of cleaning spray hanging in the air.

'Give me a hand with the recycling, Dan,' she said, and we carried the bottles out the back door together.

I finally found a clean pair of Joe's shorts under a pile of Dad's rumpled shirts.

'Finally!'

I took the stairs two at a time. 'Here we go, Joe. Joe?'

I was afraid to ask Granny. I searched all the rooms upstairs. Then I scanned downstairs without saying a word. He was nowhere to be seen.

Not again! Why does everything go pear-shaped as soon as Mam goes away? Yes, he sometimes goes missing. But not every day. Not like this. Or maybe it's just that there's normally so many of us watching out. And now there's only me. And we're used to locking doors and closing the gate – you don't even have to ask.

Closing the gate! We forgot to close the gate! I ran back upstairs and looked out the window. Sure enough the front gate was open. I didn't know where to start. Close the gate or scan the fields? I was torn. I ran downstairs and out to the gate.

Nadia was sitting on the wall opposite, still as a statue, like a cat. Her silent eyes followed me to the gate.

'I can't find Joe,' I said.

'I thought he was in respite?' She jumped down from the wall.

'He was … It's a long story – can you help me look?' I called over my shoulder, running back to the house.

'I'll get my bike,' she said.

Granny was up to her elbows in sudsy water.

'I can't find Joe,' I said. She kept scrubbing; she was trying to get the dirt off the oven trays.

'I'm sure he'll turn up,' she said. 'Did you try the garden?'

I opened and closed my mouth like a goldfish. *Did you try the garden?!*

It's not enough! We need one person on the road at least. The gate was open!

'Granny, we need to search for him,' I said.

She looked at me. 'My, my, he does give you the runabout, doesn't he?' she said.

117

'Will *you* drive down to Mr Maloney's yard?' I asked. 'Nadia can go up the road on her bike. I'll try the field.'

Granny wiped her sudsy hands on a tea towel. 'Right you are, Dan,' she said. 'Let's do this. Which way do you think he's gone?'

'I've no idea,' I said. 'I'm going to scan the fields now.'

I tried back and front, training the binoculars over every spot, but I couldn't see cattle running anywhere. It didn't mean he wasn't there, though.

Nadia was at the door. I called out the window to her. 'Will you head up to Turners'? Granny's going down the road to the farm.'

I watched as Nadia flew out the gate, her legs spinning, long hair in a black streak behind her.

Granny started up the car and turned in the opposite direction. I searched the garden again, then closed the gate and headed down the road and climbed into Mr Maloney's fields. The rain started just as I was trekking down the first field. Typical. Too late I realised I was wearing my good Nike runners. There was just no time to think.

The cows were way down at the bottom of the field, near the woods. They must have felt the rain coming. I was cursing Gorilla Face as I walked. Thinking of all the ways I'd like to flatten him into mush. The muddier my runners got, the more I wanted to stamp his hairy face into the muck.

The rain started to come down heavier. I hadn't even brought a raincoat. I was getting really sodden. I started giving out about Joe then, calling his name angrily across the field. But there was no-one there. Just the sleepy-eyed cows munching on grass, giving me dirty looks for encroaching on their peace. They flicked their tails and stumbled out of the way, occasionally lifting a tail to shoot out a long stream of green poo. I wondered if they did it deliberately to put me off.

By the time I reached the end of the field I was knackered. And there was no sign of Joe. A group of cows was huddled by the edge of the woods, sheltering from the rain. No-one was chasing them today. The rain dripped down through the leaves in soft patters. I stood and sheltered for a bit – no point in getting completely destroyed.

If I hadn't been so stressed, it would have been peaceful. I love the sound of rain dripping in the woods. The cows made little clouds of mist with their breath in the damp air. I left them to it and started trekking back uphill.

Nadia was back on the road, talking to Philip in his blue Micra.

'I hear the young lad is gone missing,' he said.

I nodded. Too tired to speak. I had a stitch in my side from running through the field.

'I'll do the loop,' he said.

'Thanks.'

'Where to now?' Nadia asked, following me back to the house, pushing her bike.

Granny came towards us from around the bend. She pulled into the drive and got out. 'Any luck?'

I shook my head.

'Frank is searching the farmyard,' she said.

'Who's Frank?'

'Mr Maloney.'

'Oh. Great. Joe loves the yard. He might show up there. You'd better stay here,' I said to Granny when we got to the house. 'We'll take the bikes.'

We went indoors and I grabbed my backpack from the hall.

'I've Kit's phone with me,' I said. I wrote down the number for her on a piece of paper. 'If he comes back here call us right away.'

Nadia looked at me. 'You have Kit's phone?' She raised her eyebrows.

I didn't answer. I grabbed a dry top and a raincoat. 'D'you want a coat?' I asked.

She nodded and took one of Kit's. 'What time are they getting back?' she asked.

'I don't know, later on today?'

I couldn't remember exactly what time they'd said. Back from the wedding in Italy. Joe gone missing. He's supposed to be in respite. Brian will be wondering what's going on. He's supposed to be there until tomorrow. He could be on the road. He could be anywhere. Think … Think … where would he go?

'Which way?' Nadia said. 'Left or right?'

I looked up and down the road. There was no blue T-shirt moving anywhere.

'Right,' I said. 'Philip is gone the loop. We'll go towards town. But keep an eye on the fields. He could be anywhere. He doesn't like the road.'

The rain had mostly stopped – there was just a thin drizzle falling as we cycled off together. At the top of our road, Mrs

Turner's yappy dog, Maisie, chased us all the way to the cross and onto the main road.

'Go home!' Nadia called, waving in her general direction. She picked up a small stick and threw it as far back as she could, so Maisie would chase after it and leave us in peace. It worked. Maisie turned and yapped after the stick, beside herself with excitement.

'That dog is a hazard on the road,' Nadia said.

I laughed. She sounded like my mother.

We cycled along the main road for about half a mile.

The wind was whizzing past my ears sailing downhill. If it wasn't for the fact that we were searching for Joe, this could have been a fun adventure.

'Do you think he'd have come this far?'

'I don't know.'

It never usually comes to this – we always find him in the field or before he's gone too far on the road. This is what Mam is always afraid of, but now she wasn't there to be afraid. I wondered if I should call and tell her. But what would I say?

'How come you have Kit's phone?' Nadia asked.

'She left it behind.'

'Did you read her messages?'

I raised my eyebrows at her and tapped my nose.

We reached the outskirts of the town without meeting anyone. The road was dead quiet.

'Why don't we double back,' Nadia suggested, 'and try the Dark Road on the way home?'

I nodded. I didn't know what to say. I looked at the

phone, but there was nothing. Clearly he hadn't wandered back home. We were just turning round and I was fixing the gears to go back uphill when my chain made a crunchy sound.

'My chain's off.'

We pulled over to the side of the road and I turned the bike upside down. It's the best way I know to get it back on properly. When I was finished I opened the backpack and washed my hands with the water and tissues. I fished out two of the snack bars. 'Hungry?' I asked.

'You come prepared,' she said, smiling.

'I learned from the best,' I replied, thinking of Joe and the bus the day before. I hadn't had time to tell her that one yet. Nadia loves to hear the latest instalments of Joe-a-rama.

We doubled back and cycled the route towards home. At the new housing estate, we got off the bikes and searched around the green.

At the cross, Philip passed us in the Micra. He put down the window. 'Frank is gone across to the far fields on his quad,' he said. 'I'll do the Dark Road. Why don't you go back towards the town?'

We've just come from there, I thought. *What's the point in going back? Would he ever get that far? It's always the cows he's after. Think… think…*

But I couldn't think of anything else to do.

'Let's go, Dan.' Nadia spun her bike around and we headed off again.

I cycled up ahead of her on the path. I didn't want her to see me upset.

'We'll find him, Dan,' she said, talking to my back. Her radar eyes can see through skulls – I'm sure of it.

We made our way along the cycle path. At the next cross Nadia stopped and stared down Mulberry Lane.

'What is it?' I asked, skidding to a stop beside her.

'We could do with your binoculars now,' she said. 'I thought I saw someone coming out of the hedge down there.' I looked where she was pointing. A yellow car cut across my view and zoomed up the back road towards town.

'Will we go take a look?'

'Could he have come all this way?' she asked.

Could he? I wondered. *Maybe… I doubt it… but we can't just stop looking. What would we do then? Call Mam?*

'Maybe…' I said.

I realised she was hesitating. Not much scares Nadia but, admittedly, Mulberry Lane is a bit creepy. Everyone at school calls it Creepy Lane and every Hallowe'en we come here and dare each other to climb the broken tree or break into the old lady's house.

The old lady's house is towards the end of the lane where the back road cuts across to town. There really was an old lady – she's not made up. Dad remembers her. But she died a long time ago and nobody looked after her house. All the windows are broken and some are boarded up. The garden is overgrown with hogweed and nettles, so you have to be careful creeping around or your skin ends up blistered and scarred with red streaks. The back window is the easiest one to get in; it leads into the sitting room. There's no furniture but the fireplace is still there. The walls are peeling with faded flowery wallpaper. In one of the bedrooms there's a rotten old mattress and the kitchen has cracked-up cupboards with chipped and broken cups.

Everyone in school says the house is haunted. Dad says it's a rumour to keep the vandals away. Kit says, 'It's just boring – who would want to go there?' But I know for a fact that she and Tanya lit a fire in the grate once. It nearly set the chimney on fire and Dad had to go and rescue them. They were planning to toast marshmallows but instead they toasted Tanya's fringe. That's what Dad told Nadia's mum the next day. I'm not supposed to know but I heard them talking when I was playing in the shed. Tanya was on a sleepover in our place when they snuck off on their adventure. For weeks afterwards Tanya had a tiny pointy fringe sticking out from her forehead.

Nadia turned her wheel in the direction of Mulberry Lane. 'It's silly the way everyone says it's haunted,' she said. 'Isn't it?'

'Totally silly,' I said. 'Let's just take a quick look.'

'D'you remember Tanya's fringe?' she asked.

We laughed about Tanya's tiny fringe as we spun down towards the broken tree. Just before the ruined house, the massive beech tree stands like a leafy mansion. One of the thickest branches split off years ago in a storm. It makes an excellent spooky cavern underneath.

Nadia stopped when we reached the tree. 'Maybe we should climb up and scan the fields,' she suggested.

'Good idea.'

We left the bikes against the wall and climbed up onto the broken branch. Nadia is like a monkey when it comes to trees. In no time at all she was up in the crook of the trunk looking out over the fields.

'I can't see anyone,' she said. Then she squeaked: 'Oh, wait, there's someone moving, someone running over there.' She pointed.

My heart leapt. I shifted closer along the branch to see out between the leaves. I twisted my foot round to keep hold but suddenly, before I knew what had happened, I was falling.

Down...

Fast...

I clipped the side of the broken branch, grabbed at the ivy, but it came away in my hand. Then I was crashing over the wall and onto the pavement below with a nasty splat.

When I opened my eyes Nadia was there, peering at me. Her black eyes had that tragic look, like I was an injured bird lying in her garden.

I tried to shake my head. 'Don't,' I said. My voice came out faint, like a whisper.

She pulled away. 'Don't what? Are you OK? Am I hurting you?'

She wasn't even touching me.

I tried to laugh but it hurt. Everything hurt. I closed my eyes again. 'Don't give me that look,' I mumbled.

'What look? Dan? Are you OK?'

I tried to sit up. 'I'm fine,' I said.

'We should call your granny.'

'Are you kidding? We call no-one. I'm fine.'

'You banged your head on the wall.'

'Did I?' No wonder it hurt so badly.

'And your arm.'

I lifted my head and looked at my arm. It was splayed out on the ground beside me.

'And your leg – your leg is cut.'

There was blood streaking down my leg. I groaned.

'Can you move your arm?' she asked.

I wiggled it gently. 'Yes, it hurts, but I can move it.'

'Good, it's not broken then. Can you sit up?'

She crouched behind and eased me up. I sat propped against the wall while she walked away.

'Where are you going?'

'Back in a sec,' she said.

She grabbed the backpack from the bike and tipped the contents onto the ground in front of us. She handed me the water bottle. 'Drink!'

There was a pack of Chewits. She peeled one open. 'Eat this,' she said. 'It'll help with the shock.'

I made a don't-be-a-drama-queen face at her but it was true. After the water and the sweets, I felt half-normal again. I tried to stand up.

Then I remembered Joe. The reality of it all hit me again and my legs wobbled. I plonked back on the ground in despair. He could be anywhere. My brother was lost. And Mam was on her way back from Italy.

'What time is it?' My voice was croaky. My throat was tight. My watch was cracked.

Nadia ignored the question. 'Let's get you cleaned up. Your granny will do her nut if she sees you like this,' she said.

She helped me back to standing and walked us slowly along the path.

'Where are we going?'

'There's a bench down here,' she said

'At the haunted house?'

'Yes, it's just here.'

She pushed in the rusted gate and sat me on the old bench. She emptied the rest of the water bottle over my leg and used the tissues to clean it up. It took a while. It was covered in dirt and bits of ivy. Underneath the greenery was a long cut.

'How's your arm?'

'Better. It's sore, though. I must have given it a right bang.'

'That's what I'm trying to tell you!' she said. 'You did a horrible flip over the wall. And you whacked your head and your arm when you landed. You're lucky it's not broken.'

'Thanks, Doctor N. Any more of those Chewits?'

She gave us one each. We sat on the bench chewing and recovering.

'He could be anywhere by now,' I said sadly, flexing my arm in and out, stretching my leg. 'I hope nothing bad's happened.'

I was afraid to say out loud what I was really thinking, the pictures that were flashing across my mind. Joe lying on the road. Joe falling down a well.

'We can't know for sure,' said Nadia, chewing her fingernail thoughtfully. 'It's better not to think terrible things; you only make it worse. Joe always comes good – we've always found him before.'

She was right. I had to stop telling crazy stories in my head. It wasn't helping.

'My dad used to bring me here,' she said then.

'Your dad? Did he?'

'When we lived in town. Before he died and we moved to our house now. We used to pick buttercups over there in the spring.' She pointed at a shady green patch across the road.

'He looks fun in the photograph,' I said. 'He has a big smile.'

'He was really fun,' she said. 'When he picked buttercups, he held them under my chin to see if it went yellow. It means you like butter. My chin was always bright yellow,' she said, 'and I do love butter.'

'Too true,' I agreed. Whenever Nadia makes a sandwich, she layers the butter on in slabs. Dad calls her the butter monster. 'I thought you didn't want to come down here because of the house.'

'I don't mind the house,' she said, 'but it reminds me of my dad, this road. Sometimes that's a happy thing, but it can be a sad thing too. I had to check to see which it is today.'

'So which is it today?' I asked, rubbing my arm. It was starting to come back to life.

'A happy thing,' she said, handing us each another Chewit. 'I'm sure he's helping to find Joe.'

'Happy days,' I said. 'We need all the help we can get.'

Nadia nodded. Her teeth were stuck together.

'It smells sweet here.' I realised that, sitting back against the bench. 'Why does it smell so sweet?'

Nadia looked around behind us. 'Elderflowers,' she said happily. 'After we find Joe, we could come back and pick them to make cordial.'

'Good idea! I love that smell. It smells like summer.'

I was starting to feel like myself again. Then I jolted back to reality. *Joe loves elderflower cordial. After we find Joe ... Joe! What am I doing sitting here?*

Nadia saw my face change. 'Let's get this show back on the road,' she said, jumping up. 'Do you think you can cycle?'

She walked back to the tree and somehow managed to wheel the two bikes to the gate. I got up and tried the bike. My legs worked OK but I really couldn't lean on my arm at all.

'My arm is banjaxed,' I said. 'It needs longer to recover.'

'Well, it's too slow with one of us walking. You can ride on the back,' she said.

'No way,' I grumbled. 'I'll be too heavy.'

I hated the idea of being carried on the back, but I knew she was right. The other alternative was to call Granny and there was no way I was doing that. Anyway, there's no stopping Nadia when she gets an idea in her head.

In the end we took my bike because it has a carrier on the back. She hid her bike inside the gate behind the gnarly elder tree.

We trundled slowly down the lane and took the back road into town. Nadia has strong legs from all the running and climbing, but even so I tried to sit lightly, to imagine myself weightless, an astronaut spinning around the moon, as she churned the pedals over and over, edging us closer to town. And hopefully closer to Joe.

We were almost at Mick's garage when I had an idea.

'Nadia?'

'What is it?'

'Can you stop? I need to check the phone.'

She pulled over ungracefully and we stumbled awkwardly onto the footpath.

'What is it?' she asked.

'Well, I've been thinking, about Gorilla Face – you know, Tommy K. He's meeting Kit – I mean, he thinks he's meeting Kit, but as I've got her phone ...'

Nadia sighed. 'What did you do, Dan?'

'Nothing. Honestly. Nothing, Nadia, yet. I just thought if I could get him to be somewhere ... we could, you know, stage an ambush?'

Nadia arched her eyebrows and gave me *the look*.

Suddenly all my plans and ideas seemed ridiculous. What was I going to do, really – throw a wet sock at his face? Swing my banjaxed arm in his general direction? Duck?

'Dan, Joe is missing. So what about that guy? Just forget it.'

'But you don't understand. He's such a creep ... he's such a mean, horrible –'

Nadia was rooting in the backpack. 'Dan ...'

'I know, it's just ... he's such a creep.'

'Dan! Not that. The phone isn't in here!'

'What? Of course it is. I put it in myself.'

'What about after you fell?' she asked miserably. 'Remember? I emptied out the bag, on the ground.'

'Oh, no.'

I felt my legs sliding away again. *Oh no-no-no-no-no-no-no-no-no-no-no-no.*

Now, let's be clear. I love my brother. But having to face my sister without her phone? I'd rather face dragons. Fire-breathing ten-ton monsters, yes. Not my sister!

'It must be on the ground, near where you fell.'

'We have to go back.' I was rooted to the spot with horror. 'What about Joe?'

'It takes too long with two of us. You go back, Nadia, and I'll walk.'

'We're only halfway to town, and you're limping,' she said.

'Do you have any better ideas?'

She shook her head sadly. 'I'm sorry,' she said in a small voice. 'If I hadn't emptied the bag…'

Nadia hates making mistakes. She gets really cross with herself. But Mam says mistakes are how you learn. She has a big sticker on the fridge that says *I ♥ mistakes*. Which is just as well really. You wouldn't want to have too high expectations in our house.

'You had more important things on your mind. You were afraid I was hurt,' I told her. 'It's not your fault. Go. I'll only be a bit further on – you're a whizz on your own. You'll be back in a few minutes.'

She was off like a shot.

Somehow it didn't feel as much of an adventure without Nadia there. I rambled along the footpath, breathing the gritty air and wondering where Mam was now. If she would see this as a mistake too, or something bigger. Like a disaster.

131

Joe was lost. Kit's phone was lost. Mam, Dad and Kit were only gone for a few days and everything had gone wrong. I walked along the kerb trying to be focused and motivated but feeling more and more like my stomach was sinking into my runners.

A car raced by, sending me wobbling in its wake. It screeched noisily and pulled in to the garage just beside me. I recognised it immediately. Ray's dad's red Hyundai. Gorilla Face and his slimeball mates.

I ducked into the hedge so they wouldn't see me.

Ray was filling up the car at the petrol pumps.

I peered out, watching them laughing and jostling each other. Suddenly Tommy turned away and began walking towards me, closer and closer. Could he see me? Impossible. I was crouched in the hedge – what was there to see? I hid my face and scrunched up smaller.

He stopped just nearby and there was the unmistakable sound of his jeans zipping down. Tommy Gorilla Face K was going for a whiz, only a few inches from where I was huddled in the hedge. Seriously! Could this day get any better?

I listened to the sound of his wee spattering the leaves and wished I was anywhere but there. Nadia was right. What on earth was I thinking? Kit's a big girl. If she wants to hang out with creeps, who am I to stop her? Taking the beers with Lucas, that was the best. But we didn't go looking for that – it just happened. It was the perfect move.

TK shouted something to Ray and the boys as he walked back, flexing his biceps, like the cockerel in Mr

Maloney's yard. I thought I heard Kit's name. They slammed the doors and zoomed off, spitting dust. Monsters. He was talking about Kit; he actually thought they were meeting up. What the heck time was it? My watch face was cracked and gritty. I couldn't see the little hands.

On the one hand, I wanted time to slow down because we had to find Joe before the others got home from Italy. On the other hand, I wished this day would turbo charge into next week and be a distant memory. And Joe would be right there. Beside me. Pulling on my arm, asking for eye-ceem.

'What are you doing in the hedge?'

It was Nadia.

There is no good way to emerge from a hedge. So I backed out like a fool, brushing the dirt from my knees, picking the twigs and leaves from my hair. 'How did you see me?'

She arched her eyebrows. 'Please. Fair play on the camouflage,' she laughed, 'but you're talking to a tracker extraordinaire.' She reached into her pocket. 'Here, it wasn't even scratched.'

Just as she handed over the phone, it started to ring. I nearly dropped it with the fright. 'It's ringing!'

Nadia laughed. 'It's a phone.'

'I just … Who could it be?'

The truth is, I'd never heard it ring. In all the time I'd been custodian of that phone, it hadn't rung once. Jingled, buzzed, beeped – yes, but no-one called.

'Dan! Answer it, quick!'

'Hello?'

It was Granny.

'Mrs Turner's son, he rang the house,' she said.

'Philip!' I said.

'Yes, that's the one. Says he met Mike the Bike down the Dark Road. And he'd been talking to your man of the Tierneys whose wife's first cousin was driving past not long ago when she saw a red-haired young fella on the road on his own after coming out of a gap in the hedge of Maloney's back field.'

'It's Joe!' I said, excited. 'It has to be!'

'It does sound like it,' she said. I could hear the relief in her voice. 'Seems he looked lost, so your woman pulled in to see if he was all right.'

'So where is he now?'

'Well, Mike the Bike said that your man of the Tierneys' wife's first cousin didn't know who he was and he couldn't tell her where home was. So she rang her sister, his wife. His wife is called Eva. Eva didn't know either, so she put him in the car (not Eva, the cousin) and she drove him into town. She was going to take him to the gardaí. Thank God for that,' said Granny.

'We're nearly there now,' I said. 'We can cycle over.'

'I'll meet you there,' said Granny. 'I'm just looking for the car keys.' I could hear her shuffling about the place, poking in drawers and emptying out her bag. Granny loses her car keys all the time.

'He's at the garda station,' I said to Nadia.

'Let's go.'

Nadia pedalled like the clappers into town. Left at the Spar, around by the scouts' hall and down to the garda station.

There was no-one there. We stood looking at the opening hours.

'It's closed,' she said.

'But this is an emergency!' I said. 'Where would they have gone?'

'I'll go around by the church,' Nadia said. 'I'll be quicker on my own. You go down that way, by Main Street. Someone must have seen them.'

We split up and she cycled off. My leg was stiff. I hobbled along the pavement keeping an eye out for anyone I could ask.

I was coming down Main Street when I noticed Mr Peroni's door was open. *He might have seen him*, I thought. I pushed open the door and went inside. The little chime tinkled over my head.

'Hello? Mr Peroni?'

I walked back towards the jukebox, past the long tables set up for dinner with their napkins and tall glasses in neat rows. At a back table near the window someone was eating noisily. I could hear them munching then slurping loudly – on one of Mr Peroni's thick vanilla milkshakes by the sounds of it. I walked up in front of the red-leather booth.

I don't believe it!

There was Joe, sitting with a plate of chips and a huge milkshake on the table beside him.

'Joe!' I said. 'You're here!'

'Tips,' he replied, and he stuffed another six of them into his mouth at once.

My legs went weak with relief. I sat down beside him and hugged his arm. He was too focused on his chips to take any notice. Did he even realise that he'd been missing? All that running about searching and here he was, safe and sound. But how?

I looked more closely. His top was soaking wet and bits of the hedge and who knows what else were stuck in his hair. Someone had taken off his runners and they were under the radiator, drying out. You could hardly see the runners for the muck. His socks were streaked green and brown with cow poo.

I looked around for someone to talk to.

Mr Peroni came backing out of the kitchen with a stack of plates in one hand and a phone in the other. 'Ah, Dan,' he said. 'That's great timing. I was just trying to get a number for your mam.'

'Mam's in Italy,' I said. 'Or at least she was, she's due back today ... some time. Thanks so much, Mr Peroni. How did you find Joe?'

'Well, I had just popped next door to Morrissey's to buy the paper and this lady arrived, a relative of one of the Tierneys', I think.'

'The wife's first cousin,' I said.

He looked at me. 'Something like that,' he said. 'Anyway, she found Joe on the road, but she was going to a meeting so she couldn't hang around. I said, "I know this young lad. He can stay here until I call his mam."'

'Thank you so much, Mr Peroni,' I said. 'You've saved the day. How much do I owe you for the chips?'

'Don't be silly, Dan,' he said. 'It's on the house. He can have it on his tab, heh heh heh.'

'I'll need to call Granny,' I said.

When I looked around, Joe was heading out the door, milkshake in hand, his green cow-poo socks sliding off his feet, like flippers.

'Wait for me, Joe,' I called.

By the time I stumbled out the door, clutching the phone, he was already heading across the road. Luckily the little man was green. Half-way across he bent down and started crawling around, patting the ground. There was a lump of old chewing gum or something stuck to the road and he was trying to get it off.

'Joe,' I called.

Someone was coming towards him, walking the other way.

'Can you just grab –?' I called out.

Then I saw who it was. Tommy K was striding across the intersection like he owned it, talking to someone on his phone. Joe was on the ground in front of him.

'Get out of the way, ya big eejit,' he said to Joe. 'You're blocking up half the road.'

He tried to move him with his feet.

'Just a second,' he said into the phone. 'Move it, will ya?'

He thinks he's back on the training field, I thought, *the big meanie!* My belly was on fire. That's exactly what he was like that day by the river. Suddenly I was scared. There was no hedge to duck into. Would he remember about the cans when he saw me? Did he realise who took them? Who else? But I couldn't leave Joe in the middle of the road. It was all happening so fast! I was trying to unfreeze my legs when a familiar car pulled up in front of them. The passenger door sprang open and Kit was standing there.

I stepped back into Peroni's doorway. Kit didn't notice me.

'Leave him alone, Tom,' she said. 'He doesn't understand.'

Tommy K took a step back. 'Sure I was only messing with him,' he said. 'He's in the middle of the road – he's a road hazard! When did you land back?' he asked then, ignoring Joe. 'Welcome home, honey bee.' He smirked and made to put an arm around her. 'You're late. Thought you were trying to stand me up.'

Kit took a step away from him. 'Eh?' she said.

Uh-oh, I thought. I could feel her phone nestled snugly in my back pocket.

'We're just heading over to Tyler's. If you wanna come?'

She looked at him then and she looked down at Joe, still on the ground, fumbling around beside her feet. One of his socks had fallen off and he was trying to get the lid off the milkshake so he could lick the rest of it off his fingers.

She looked confused. Then she shook her head. 'Ah, no thanks,' she said.

He gave her a funny look and made to grab her arm but she stood aside.

'I said, no thanks, Tom.'

She sounded like Mam with her that's-enough-of-that voice. People were starting to drift over, curious what all the commotion was about. He backed away.

Kit bent down beside Joe, picked up the sock and the milkshake, took him by the hand and led him over to the car, and they both got in. Our car was stalled at the lights with the door open. Obviously the trip to Italy was OV-ER. The car had caused quite a bit of a traffic jam already: the lights were green and some of the cars behind were beeping and other cars had started to go around. I could see Mam waking up on the back seat. Dad was trying to manoeuvre out of the way to a better spot. Joe spotted me out the window and started waving.

'Dan, Dan, Dan!' I knew that's what he was saying. He loves that my name is so easy to say – success every time.

Mam was scanning the scene with her laser eyes, fully awake now. She spotted me lurking in the doorway and buzzed down the window.

'How was the wedding?' I asked, coming forward and stretching my mouth into a wide smile.

'What in God's name, Dan…?' She looked around, confused, trying to piece things together. 'What are you doing here? And why is Joe not in respite?'

I was waiting for that. The trillion-dollar question.

Then she had to stop talking while Dad parked the car properly. I limped beside them to the side of the road. She flung open the car door and stared up at me.

'Dan?' she asked.

I could see the panic mounting in her eyes. I was wondering where to start.

'Well,' I said, 'Granny thought we should take him out for a bit of fresh air.'

Dad got out and shut the car door with a bang. He took in the scene at a glance.

'I'm starving!' he said. 'They feed you nothing on those flights. A fiver for a sandwich the size of a postage stamp!

What about a few chips in Peroni's?'

At that exact moment, Nadia came spinning around the corner on her bike, hair flying. She braked, suddenly bopping off the kerb, when she saw us all standing there. 'You found him!' she exclaimed.

Kit looked at her curiously. 'Found who?' she asked. 'Hi, Nadia, what are you doing here?'

'Where's Granny?' Mam wondered, looking around as if she expected her to materialise from the gutter.

'Granny!' Nadia said to me. 'You'd better call your granny and let her know.'

'Da-an,' said Mam, 'what's going on? Are you limping? What happened your arm?'

I had the phone out and in my hand before I remembered.

'Hey!' said Kit. 'Is that my phone?'

'I can explain,' I muttered, backing away from her eyes, which were about to pop out of her head and land on my feet. 'But right now I just need to make a couple of calls.'

We all trooped in the door to Peroni's.

'Welcome back, my friend,' Mr Peroni said, clapping Joe on the back and shaking his hand. 'Have you not had enough to eat already? Have you come to settle your tab? Heh heh heh.' He laughed his Italian laugh.

Dad gave him a quizzical look. 'Dan?' he said.

'Can we have the table by the window, please?' I counted names on my fingers. 'We need room for nine.'

'Don't forget to call your granny,' Nadia said, sliding in behind the table. Another thing she doesn't need to remind me about.

'Nine of us?' said Mam

'We-ell, I need to call Mrs Turner's Philip and let him know we're here, and then there's Frank.'

'Who's Frank?' asked Kit.

'Mr Maloney,' I said.

'You need to let him know what?' asked Mam.

I looked at her. 'That we've found Joe,' I said.

'Ahhh,' she said. 'I see.'

'Give us nine bags of chips, please, Lorenzo,' said Dad, hugging Joe in a tight bear lock. 'Did you go wandering off again?'

'Tips,' said Joe.

Then everyone started talking at once:

'Two more milkshakes, please.'

'More of that fresh fish when you're ready.'

'Don't forget the garlic sauce,' said Kit.

'No, don't!' added Nadia. 'I'm mad for the garlic sauce.'

The chips were just on the table when Granny arrived in, mopping her forehead. Mrs Turner's Philip was close on her heels.

'How was Italy, folks?' asked Philip, giving Joe a pat on the head.

Granny looked at him with relief. 'Well, mister, you gave us all a right turn,' she said, shaking her head. 'I rang the school,' she added, to no-one in particular.

'I'll drop him over after this,' said Dad. 'We can take your car.' He nodded at Granny. 'Brian will want him back; they're rehearsing for a music show tomorrow. We're all invited.'

'I didn't know about that,' Granny said sheepishly. 'I was afraid he might be bored. Thought he'd like a little trip out.'

I saw Mam and Dad share a look but no-one said anything.

'Moosic,' Joe piped up.

We sat around the table, tucking into the mound of chips. Mr Peroni joined us for a while.

Kit had her phone back. She was scrolling slowly through the pictures. It was all coming back to me now. Alisha's pictures, from start to end. The girl with the dark hair. That's how I knew her – Francesca, Mr Peroni's daughter; she works here on the weekends.

'Francesca is having good times in Greece,' he said. As if he could read my mind. 'These girls are having a lovely relaxing holiday.'

Kit kept scrolling through the photos. She snorted and a stream of lemonade ran out her nose. She smiled at him, all teeth. 'Yes, I heard they're having a blast,' she said.

She slid the phone into her bag and glared at me. I studied Mr Peroni's new wallpaper.

'Nice wallpaper,' I told him. 'I love the green stars.'

Totally NOT MY FAULT Francesca and Alisha are living it up in bikini-land and don't know when to stop drinking cocktails or taking photos.

I felt someone kicking my leg.

'Were you looking at my photos?' Kit hissed across the table.

I shook my head innocently. 'Never!' I said. 'Wouldn't dream of it.'

I smothered a chip in garlic sauce and stuffed it in my mouth.

I went home with Nadia. I could have taken a lift but it felt right to finish it off together.

She was right. Joe always comes right. Superhero Joe. He finds the best people with his super radar. He's a superhero bro.

The rain had dried up and the sun shone, making rainbows in the puddles. We walked back to Mulberry Lane and rescued Nadia's bike from behind the gate. She filled the backpack with elderflowers. Now that we'd found Joe, my arm was suddenly fine. I could cycle. I felt like I could do anything! I pulled down my hood and let the air whistle past my ears. The sun was warm on the back of my neck. The top of our road was flooded right across to the ditch.

'Geronimo!' yelled Nadia as she tore through the middle of the puddle. Water splashed up on both sides in a big arc.

I followed behind, shouting so loud my voice was hoarse. 'Geronimooooooo!'

In no time at all we were at the gate.

'Thanks for your help,' I said. 'That was a mental day.'

She smiled. 'Happy to help. It was a team effort.'

A team effort. She's right. That's Nadia, never makes a big deal, but she's always there when you need her.

'D'you want to go for a run later?' I asked.

'Thought you'd have seen enough action for one day. Your leg was pretty banged up.'

'I dunno. I feel better now. I feel great. I feel like running, after I get something to eat.'

It's something about these summer days. I never want them to end.

She laughed. 'OK, Usain Bolt, meet you back here in a couple of hours?'

'See you then.' I started strolling back to the house.

'Don't forget your water bottle.'

ONE WEEK LATER

Joe's music show was a great success. Brian had him rocking on the bongos. I've never seen Joe keep a beat. I don't know how Brian did it. He had them all banging away in sync. They actually managed to sound good. Genuinely. It's like he waved a magic wand. For one whole half-hour they were listening, watching and playing, making a real show. It made me think – if they can do it, then so can I.

I've got a new tune dancing around my head and I've been scribbling down some lines.

Then on Saturday, I came second in the fun run. Joe ran half of it before he ran out of steam. He and Dad walked the rest of the way. He's not really a follow-the-lines type of guy; he'd rather be zig-zagging through the fields. Nadia came in sixth and set a new personal best. We sat at the finish line waiting for Dad and Joe.

'Did you write any more verses for your song?' she asked

'I've started a new one,' I said. 'It's called "My Brother the Superhero".'

She laughed. 'I'd like to hear that.'

'No joke. I've finished it already,' I said. 'It's one of the easiest songs I've ever written.'

That's no lie. Maybe the best songs just write themselves, maybe because the story is so true. I don't really have to try.

'Nothing fancy, it just works,' I said.

'Tanya says Kit's going to the debs with Mike the Bike's younger brother, Les,' Nadia said.

'Mmmmm...'

'And Francesca Peroni is going with Alisha,' she added.

'Apparently so.'

Isn't Tanya a fountain of information? Normally I really don't care, but I feel slightly proud that for once I am ahead of her in the local news. She can't surprise me with anything.

Most people think that to be a superhero you have to run faster or jump higher or invent a great thing: even rule the world or make billions...

But maybe that's not it at all.

Maybe it's just the little things.

Like if your man Tierney's wife's first cousin hadn't stopped that day on the road...

Or if Mr Peroni didn't shake hands with Joe the first time they met....

If Old Mrs Turner's son Philip hadn't turned up at the petrol pumps....

If that kind lady on the bus hadn't told me how to get off...

If Nadia wasn't always there at the gate...

If Joe didn't make people love him...

    ... not because he's perfect...
    ... but because he isn't...

... because he tugs at their hearts more and more
until there's nothing left to do but love him and
love him
          and love him
          even more.

Maybe that's his superpower.

EPILOGUE

Kit was down the garden stoking a little fire. She was sitting on an old mossy branch feeding a stack of multi-coloured sticky notes to the jumping flames. Joe was circling around playing with one of his sticks. The air smelled of roses and smoke. I could hear pigeons cooing in the beech tree behind her. I walked over and added one of the sticky notes to the fire.

'Guess you don't need them any more.'

She smiled. 'Guess I don't.'

'Start of a new adventure, Kit.'

'For you too. How are you feeling about secondary school, Dan?'

I looked down at the ground.

'That bad?' She patted the log beside her. 'Come and sit down.'

I sat down beside her and she took my whole arm and nuzzled it in a hug. I love the way she does that.

'Ah, Dan.'

I felt warm and fuzzy inside.

This is the Kit I remember. Before exams swallowed her up, before the rows over who does what at home, before Gorilla Face.

'It's going to be crap,' I said. 'What if I hate it there? What if Mac the Monster is my maths teacher?'

What if everyone laughs at me?
What if I can't do the work?
What if I miss the bus?
What if ..?.

'I know exactly the feeling, Dan,' she said. 'I'm excited about going to college, but I'm terrified too. I'm sad to be leaving everyone, but at the same time I can't wait to get away.'

I felt a bag of tears building up behind my eyes. 'I'll miss you.'

'I'll miss you too.'

'Can I have your comic collection?'

'Sure.'

'At least I'll have Lucas,' I said. 'Lucas is sound.'

'Lucas and his leather jacket,' she said.

We laughed.

'And Nadia will be there,' she said.

'True, Nadia will be there,' I agreed.

She gave me a sideways look, but she didn't say anything.

Joe threw his stick into the hedge and a terrified crow came squawking out. He jumped back with a fright and we both laughed again.

'There's so many kids in that school,' I said.

'I know, it's a big change. I was terrified my first day.'

'Were you?'

'Absolutely shitting a brick.'

I laughed. I can't imagine Kit terrified. Terrifying, maybe... 'I'm sorry about Tommy K.'

'Don't be,' she said. 'He was a bad egg.'

She sounded so much like Granny. We looked at each other and burst into fits of laughing. It was one of those fits where the more we laughed, the more we kept on laughing. I had tears rolling down my face from laughing. Every time we looked at each other, we were off again.

Finally, when we had laughed ourselves stupid, she threw the last of her notes in the fire and stood up.

'Come on.' She held out her hand. 'Will you help me make the dinner? It's fish pie – I found the recipe in one of Granny's old books.'

I took her hand and she pulled me up.

'We're going to make dinner, Joe,' I said. 'Are you coming?'

'Tips,' he answered hopefully as he wandered towards the back door.

Kit poked at the papers quickly turning into ash. A little plume of grey-blue smoke curled into the sky. 'Bye bye, old,' she said. 'Hello, new.'

She smiled at me. Then she took my arm and we walked back up to the house together to start the dinner.

Acknowledgements

Huge thanks to Siobhán Parkinson, Matthew Parkinson-Bennett and all at Little Island who gave their support and feedback, bringing this book to life.

My gratitude and appreciation to all at the Tyrone Guthrie Centre at Annaghmakerrig – a creative wellspring where I've found peace, inspiration and productivity. The warmhearted staff, beautiful surroundings and artistic community I've met there are a rich source of nourishment.

I'm also very grateful to the Arts Council for their encouragement and assistance in various projects over the years that have led me, eventually, to this book.

To Rachael Hegarty for your editorial eagle eye, humour, camaraderie and friendship these many years as trusty writing partner. I am ever thankful.

To my many friends and colleagues, for your support and encouragement every step of the way in my unfolding creative journey, thank you!

Though the characters and setting of this book are fictional, it is based on my experiences growing up with a brother with special needs. I'm very grateful to my brother for all he taught us during his life and to my parents and siblings for the rich and sacred journey together. To all of those who supported him and us during those years, our extended family, friends, neighbours, local community, his school and social support system, I offer my heartfelt gratitude.

For their constant, unyielding love and colourful company – my husband Martin and my children Meadhbh and Dían – my well-wishers, my joy.

Le grá
Siobhán

Music

In this book, Dan loves writing songs and playing them on his guitar. Writing songs helps him to talk about what's going on in his life, especially the tricky things.

Have you ever wanted to write your own songs?

What would you like to write about?

If you'd like to hear Dan's songs played on guitar, see what chords he uses and get some ideas for making your own songs, visit:

www.siobhandaffy.com/noordinaryjoe
or
www.littleisland.ie

Special thanks to Mark Ellison for his musical skills and collaborative spirit in bringing these lyrics to life.

We hope you have enjoyed reading *No Ordinary Joe*. On the following pages you will find out about some other Little Island books you might like to read.

Little Island

WOLFSTONGUE
By Sam Thompson
Illustrated by Anna Tromop

Deep in the Forest, the foxes live in an underground city built by their wolf slaves. The foxes' leader Reynard controls everything with his clever talk.

At school, Silas is getting bullied because his words will not come. He wishes he could live in silence as animals do.

Then Silas meets an injured wolf and helps him. Isengrim, Hersent and their pups are the only wolves left, moving between the human and animal worlds using hidden passageways as they fight to survive.

When Silas enters the secret world of the Forest he will learn that, even here, language is power. Can he find his voice in time to help his wolf friends – can he become the Wolfstongue?

'An edge-of-the-seat adventure.' – Meg Rosoff
'An unforgettable fable.' – Lucy Strange
'A highly original story, warm and thoughtful, full of insight.'
– Kelly McCaughrain
'Heartwarming and brave.' – Myra Zepf
'Wolfstongue has modern classic written all over it.' – Patricia Forde

MY SECRET DRAGON
By Debbie Thomas

Aidan Mooney has the mother of all problems. His mother is part-dragon.

He's spent his whole life struggling to keep her hidden from the world. But now, with the help of his super-smart new friend Charlotte, Aidan discovers a much darker secret hiding in the woods...

Loneliness, isolation, anxiety and being different are explored in this tender and heartwarming tale. A mother-son relationship and friendship between a boy and girl are at the heart of the story. And at the end – fun baking recipes to try at home!

'A smashing romp. The writing is excellent.'
– Celine Kiernan, author of *Begone the Raggedy Witches*

'Unforgettable characters and page-turning action.'
– E.R. Murray, author of the Book of Learning trilogy

A DANGEROUS CROSSING

By Jane Mitchell

Ghalib doesn't want to leave his home, but Syria has become too dangerous, and his family has no choice but to flee. Together they start out on a terrible journey that leads them through dark and dangerous places. They come under fire; they are fleeced by illegal border-breakers; they experience the wretched and hopeless life of a refugee camp. And they still have to face the perils of a voyage in a boat that is far from seaworthy.

Based on the experiences of real Syrian families, *A Dangerous Crossing* is a story of bravery and solidarity in the face of despair.

'Deserving of a place on every school reading list.' – BookTrust UK

Recommended by Amnesty International

About the Author

Siobhán Daffy worked as a creative arts facilitator in community arts for over twenty years with children, adults, women's groups and people with physical and intellectual disabilities. She is a lover of creative fire and self-expression and believes strongly in the power of artistic expression for self-development and social change.

Siobhán is a poet and performance artist. Her poems have been published in many journals and magazines, and she enjoys performing at festivals and events. In 2016 she released a CD called *Horses Hooves*, a collaboration of spoken poetry and music, with six musicians from Ireland and the UK.

Siobhán is also a natural health practitioner @natural_rhythms and runs a busy practice online and onsite, focusing on women's emotional and hormonal health.

This is her first children's novel.

About Little Island

Founded in 2010 in Dublin, Ireland, Little Island Books publishes good books for young minds, from toddlers all the way up to older teens. In 2019 Little Island won a Small Press of the Year award at the British Book Awards. As well as publishing a lot of new Irish writers and illustrators, Little Island publishes books in translation from around the world.

www.littleisland.ie